Praise for Gary Reilly and *The Asphalt Warrior*

"Reilly is a master wordsmith."

—*The Denver Post*

"Gary Reilly proves himself to be not just a gifted stylist, but a kind of Jedi Master of the understated."

—Fred Haefele, author of *Extremeophilia*

"Any cabbie that quotes Nabokov's *Lolita* … uses a copy of *Finnegans Wake* as a piggy bank, ruminates on English Romanticism [and runs] everything through a screwy sixties TV sitcom filter debating its intellectual value, well, I'll ride with that guy."

—Barry Wightman, author of forthcoming *Pepperland*

"If Murph doesn't win your heart, it can't be won."

—Mark Graham, co-author of *The Natanz Directive*

"I found Murph to be laugh-out-loud and consistently funny, yet life-smart and grudgingly loveable."

—Kathy Lynn Harris, author of *The Blue Straggler*

"An intriguing and interesting read."

—*Taxitalk Magazine*

TICKET TO HOLLYWOOD

A NOVEL

GARY REILLY

Running Meter Press

DENVER

Published by
Running Meter Press
2509 Xanthia St.
Denver, CO 80238
Publisher@RunningMeterPress.com
720 328 5488

Cover art by John Sherffius

ISBN: 978-0-9847860-1-5

Library of Congress Control Number: 2012948419

First Edition 2013

Printed in the United States of America

CHAPTER 1

I had just dropped off a fare at a bar on east Colfax when a call came over the radio for an address on Capitol Hill. The customer wanted to go to Larimer Square. I snatched the microphone off the dash and said, "One twenty-seven." With luck I might make five more bucks before quitting time. It was winter, it was dark, and I wanted to go home, but I took the call because driving a cab is like playing a slot machine: when you win, you win money.

The dispatcher gave me an address for an apartment building on 14th Avenue. I had picked up fares there before. Young people. Students. Punks. Losers. Unemployed. My kind of people. As soon as I pulled up at the curb, the foyer door opened and a young woman came out dressed like a flapper. It didn't take F. Scott Fitzgerald to tell me where she was going: the Mile-Hi Film Festival. Bigwigs from Hollywood always attended the festival. I was looking forward to having a bigwig in the backseat of my taxi, but bigwigs rode in limousines. I didn't blame them. If I was a bigwig I would go first class, too. But realistically speaking, the odds of me ever becoming a bigwig are six-to-one.

As soon as she climbed into the backseat I smelled vodka. During the brief moment that the overhead light was on, I noted that my fare was probably eighteen, but the dress made her look nineteen. It was white, tight, and short. She was wearing a flapper cap. She was clutching a beaded purse. Strings of pearls were draped around her neck. She threw herself into a reclining position and leaned her head against the far door and said, "I want to go to … you know … that place downtown."

Smirnoff Vodka, if I wasn't mistaken, and I usually wasn't.

"The Flicker?" I said.

A wide smile elbowed its way between her cheeks. "How did you know?" she said.

I knew because that's where *The Great Gatsby* was showing. I had browsed through the film festival schedule over the weekend, making red checkmarks next to the movies I didn't want to see.

"A lucky guess," I said. "You look like Zelda Fitzgerald."

"Who?" she said.

I dropped my flag and pulled away from the curb. I had the feeling this was going to be a long five minutes.

"She was a flapper," I said. "She was married to the guy who wrote *The Great Gatsby.*"

"Don't you just love that movie?" she said.

"Love ain't the word."

"I've seen it fourteen times," she said.

"That's a lot of times to see a movie," I said. "Did you ever read the book?"

"What book?"

I swallowed hard.

"*The Great Gatsby,*" I said. "It's a novel."

"Really?" she said. "I've never read a novel. I'm an actress."

I opened my mouth to say something, but nothing came out. In my entire life I had never heard two sentences like that uttered consecutively. We rode in silence for a bit, then I heard her moving in the backseat. She was sitting up. I looked at the rear-view mirror and saw her leaning toward the front seat. She rested her arms on the seatback.

"Do you know him?" she said.

"Know who?"

"The guy who wrote that book."

"He died a long time ago."

"Oh," she said. "I thought maybe you were friends with him."

I was wrong. It was Gilbey's, not Smirnoff. I suddenly realized she was carrying a half-pint in her purse. I realized it when she pulled it out and held it in front of my nose.

"Want a drinkie?" she said.

I raised my hand and eased the bottle out of my line of vision. I'm a beer man. "Aren't you a little young to be drinking vodka?"

She pouted and flopped back against the seat. "You sound like my faaaaather," she said. She unscrewed the cap and took a snort.

This made me feel bad. It reminded me of college. But that was long ago and in another time zone.

We came to Lincoln Boulevard. I made a right turn toward midtown. I glanced at her in the mirror and said, "It's kind of cold out. Don't you have a coat?"

She took another drink and put the booze away. "I don't need a coat where I'm going."

"Where are you going?"

"To a party. They're having a costume party after the movie."

I had the urge to counter her logic, but I was talking to a drunk person. I had wended my way through conversations with plenty of drunks before, but never one this young, at least not as a cab driver. College is another story. "Are you meeting friends there?" I said.

She started giggling. "Yes, daddy, I'm meeting friends there."

"Are they actors, too?" I said.

She frowned at me. "Why do you keep asking me so many quesssstions?"

I ran her tone of voice and facial expression through the Univac inside my brain. It spit out a card that said ease off. Her life was none of my business. My rule-of-thumb is to never get involved in the personal lives of my fares. My success rate is about as big as my thumb.

"Just making conversation," I said. "Acting interests me. Driving a cab is sort of like being an actor. And I had friends in college who were actors. I know a lot of people who aren't what they seem to be."

"You went to college?" she said.

"I graduated fifteen years ago," I said.

"Did you major in cab driving?" she said, and burst out laughing.

I'll admit it. She zinged me. I filed her quip in my mental Rolodex under P for plagiarism. I know a keeper when I hear one.

I grinned and said, "Nah, I was an English major."

"Is that how come you know so much about books?" she said.

"That's how come," I replied.

I slowed for the light at 18th Avenue. The Flicker was a small art theater in Larimer Square at 15th. I was forced by downtown Denver's spectacular one-way street system to circle three blocks out of my way and come at it from the north. They were showing a lot of F. Scott Fitzgerald movies at The Flicker that week. God knows why. Maybe because Hemingway refused to write screenplays. William Faulkner didn't refuse though. He sold out plenty of times. That's one of the two things I like most about Faulkner. The other is Flem Snopes.

"Your ponytail is cute," she said.

"Thanks."

"Are you a hippie?"

"No."

"You look like a hippie."

"That's part of my act. Like I always say, there's no business like show business except cab driving. Role-playing is crucial. If I looked like the kind of person I really am, I would never get tips."

"I love acting."

"What kind of acting do you do?"

"I had the lead role in my high school play."

"Yeah? What play was that?"

"*Carousel.*"

"*Carousel,*" I said. I didn't know what else to say.

"I sang in it," she said.

"Are you a good singer?"

"I am a very good singer," she said. "My teacher told me so. Mr. Delrubio said I should be on Broadway."

I thought about this as The Flicker came into view. The world is full of Mr. Delrubios. I have a few Delrubios tucked away in a steamer trunk in my apartment. But I decided not to comment on Mr. Delrubio. Having never met the guy personally, I did not feel it appropriate to pass judgment on what I naturally assumed was bad advice. I assume all advice is bad, even my own.

I stopped at the red light at 15th and Larimer, and suddenly the girl in the backseat started singing. She sang very quietly and very melodiously:

"... Off you will go in the mist of day, never ever to know, how I loved you ..." and she stopped.

I waited for her to sing "... soooo ..." but she didn't.

It wasn't until sometime later that I learned that Rogers and Hammerstein hadn't given that lyric a so.

The light turned green. I pulled the cab forward and parked at the curb outside The Flicker. There was a crowd of people waiting in line to get into the movie. "Six-forty," I said, pointing directly at my taximeter.

The girl leaned forward and squinted at the meter. Then she reached down the front of her dress and pulled out a ten-dollar bill and handed it to me.

"Keep the change, Charley," she said with giggle.

"Thanks," I said.

She opened the door and got out, closed it, and walked toward the throng waiting to see Robert Redford's portrayal of Scott Fitzgerald's gold-hatted high-bouncing lover. I waited to see if anyone stepped forward to greet her, but she melded with the crowd and disappeared.

She was just a kid, and I had a feeling she didn't belong where she was going, but that's true of most people. A horn honked. I looked at my rear-view mirror. A Yellow Cab was waiting to get into my space at the curb. The driver had a whole slew of gold-hatted high-bouncers in his hack. I took one last look at the throng on the sidewalk, then I put my cab into gear and pulled away from the curb.

If it hadn't been so close to the end of my shift, I would have cruised along Larimer Square looking to pick up a pedestrian or two. Normally I don't deal with pedestrians hailing cabs on the street. Denver isn't like New York City where people are always flagging taxis and riding eight blocks. I don't know how the cabbies in New York City make it. I've never been to New York. Whenever I see a movie set in New York, the streets look like a river of Yellow Cabs. Before I started driving a cab, I had never taken notice of them on the streets of Denver, but after I got my license I started seeing taxis everywhere. The competition looked stiff. I hate competition. It's one of the seven warning signs of work. I've spent most of my life trying to figure out ways to make money without working. I don't know what I could do to get money besides driving a cab, except robbing banks. Both occupations have their pros and cons. For instance, bank robbery isn't quite as dangerous as cab driving, but it pays better.

I made my way back over to Broadway, leaving the glitz and glamour of Hollywood behind me. As much as I tried not to, I hoped the girl would be okay. As I said, I avoid getting involved in the personal lives of my fares. As a professional cab driver it is incumbent upon me to treat my customers the same way a doctor treats his patients: keep them alive long enough to get the money.

But I started thinking about *The Great Gatsby*. I first read it when I was a junior at the University of Colorado at Denver, which is, ironically, three blocks away from The Flicker. It's an urban school spread over a few blocks of downtown. *Gatsby* was assigned to my English class, but on the day we were due to discuss it, the teacher found out that practically nobody had read the book. Nobody seemed to understand the symbolism of the green light at the end of Daisy's dock.

The teacher went down the rows of desks asking each student if he or she had read the book. Everyone said no. Everyone except me. I felt like a traitor. An outsider. An egghead. Fortunately I didn't understand the symbolism either, but I still felt like a pariah.

But I couldn't stop thinking about the actress who had told me she had never read a novel. Who was I to judge her? She was like an English major, the poor kid. I put her out of my mind and drove back toward the Rocky Mountain Taxicab Company (RMTC). It was quitting time. My fake weekend had begun. I always take Tuesday off, unless my rent is due and I need to pick up some extra cash. I always take Thursday off, too. I have two fake weekends and one real weekend per week. Sometimes I wish there were eight days in a week just so I could squeeze in an extra weekend. But we all have our crosses to bear.

CHAPTER 2

I had made my fifty bucks for the shift, so I was feeling good as I headed toward Rocky in the dark. The day had started out slow, but during the afternoon business had picked up due to the film festival. People were going from theater to theater, catching movies and lectures. It was January and it was cold outside. I don't know why they hold big events like that in the winter. I don't know why anybody does anything in the winter. I always say, if you want to do something, move to Phoenix.

I get a lot of businessmen in my cab who go to Phoenix just to play golf. Apparently Phoenix is a big golf town. I've never been there. Don't plan to go there. Golf baffles me. They say it's a sport, and I have to take their word for it, but anything that involves having fun while standing up doesn't interest me. That includes dancing. NASCAR I can understand. In fact, anything that involves sitting down automatically has my interest, and it doesn't have to be a sport. I've done plenty of nothing while sitting down. I even make a living at it.

After I got back to Rocky Cab, or the "motor" as we call it, I sat for a few minutes in the warmth of my taxi filling out my trip-sheet and counting my profits before going inside to turn in my key. Believe it or not, I had an itch to keep on driving, but that's only because there were more shoes on the street than usual, thanks to the film festival. Bad weather is a cab driver's best friend, and it was cold outside. The only way it could have been better was if it was snowing. The fact that I hate driving in the snow is irrelevant. I like money even more than I hate snow. Don't ask me why I live in Denver. If I ever find out I'll let you know.

I took a moment to police up the cab. This involved emptying ashtrays and collecting Twinkie wrappers and a couple of empty Coke cans lying on the floor. When business starts hopping it sometimes becomes difficult to keep the place tidy. The top brass at Rocky Cab constantly reminds us cabbies that good hygiene translates into good tips, and a clean cab is good advertising. But when you're making a dash to a restroom at a 7-11, your mind is usually focused on personal hygiene. I once thought about getting hold of a hospital urinal so I could speed things up. But I was afraid I would learn the hard way that it would prove impractical. That's how I learn almost everything.

I gathered up my trash and took a quick peek into the backseat. I rarely get fares who leave their trash behind, although they sometimes leave other things, such as cameras, books, and flapper purses. You heard me right. Resting on the floor halfway under the seat was a white purse of the type the IT girl had been carrying with her when she climbed into my cab. I froze. A scenario of depressing proportions crossed my mind. If that actually was her purse, then it meant she didn't have any money or I.D. on her, and I would be forced by ethics, if nothing else, to go back and track her down, since I knew where she was at that moment.

I reached in and picked up the purse. I gave it a heft. It did not contain a bottle of vodka. Take my word for it. I know my metric weights. But it did contain small objects. You may not believe this, but I actually hate digging through women's purses. I made that mistake once in my life and I vowed never to make it again.

I stood for a moment in the dirt parking lot of Rocky Cab faced with a quandary. If I drove straight back to The Flicker I would probably be able to find her and return the purse. But if I did that, it would mean bringing my cab in late and being embarrassed for one minute while I was charged a late fee. The gutless thing to do of course would have been to take the purse inside and hand it over to Rollo, the man in the cage. He would have put it in the lost-and-found and it would have remained there until the owner called for it. The lost-and-found was a cardboard box under Rollo's desk. It was usually empty. Don't ask me why. Ask Rollo.

That was the official procedure anyway.

But the girl apparently didn't possess any money. Then I recalled that she had pulled the sawbuck out of her bodice. Maybe that's where flappers kept their dough back in the 1920s. But I had a feeling that a girl who had never read a novel probably knew less about history than I knew about golf. The costume had a rented look. She probably had leased it that afternoon for the Gatsby party without doing a systematic study of the sociological and cultural impact of Jazz Age fashions on the banking industry. That would be my guess anyway.

I started to get irritated. It was dark and it was cold, and I had a TV waiting for me at home. I used my irritation as an excuse to open her purse. That was the same excuse I used the first time I ever opened a woman's purse—turned out I had the wrong purse. I could really use an anger management course. Let's drop it.

There was a tube of lipstick and a wad of dough in the flapper's purse. I closed it fast.

It's a funny thing about money. It's just paper, yet it throbs with a power that is both illusory and real. Illusory because it's only paper, yet real because you can buy things with it. English professors refer to this phenomenon as "symbolism." In all the English literature courses I ever slept through in college, I had never taken symbolism seriously, especially that business about Daisy's dock. Symbolism seemed like something that writers threw into their stories when they couldn't think up a plot. But as I stood there in the parking lot of Rocky Cab on that cold winter night I began to get the funny feeling I understood Proust.

I swallowed hard.

The outer bill on the wad of money had the number 100 on it. I'm talking Ben Franklin. Whoever that girl was, she was not only not broke, she was loaded. I decided it would be best to go back to The Flicker and find the girl. I felt compelled to do it. That's another funny thing about money. It compels people to do things. It even clouds men's minds. If my mind hadn't been so clouded I would have taken the purse in to Rocky Cab right then and just handed it to Rollo. But I've never trusted Rollo. His lost-and-found box is always empty.

To hell with it. I decided to drive back to The Flicker and risk one minute of embarrassment later. The girl might already be freaking out over her lost purse, except she was drunk and might not even know she had lost her money. It's been known to happen, especially to me. And who knows, maybe I would get a hefty tip. Tips are like money. They compel cabbies to do things, and it takes a lot to make me do anything.

I had five minutes left on the clock so I didn't have any illusion about making it to the movie and back in time to avoid a late fee. They charge you five bucks for every half-hour you bring your cab in late, unless the man in the cage looks the other way. Rollo had done that for me a number of times in the past, but there were no guarantees. It depended on his mood. He could be a moody guy, especially if he didn't like you. As far as I could tell, Rollo didn't like anybody.

But my irritation dissipated as I drove back toward downtown Denver. I started feeling noble. I was making a sacrifice to save a princess. That was one way of looking at it. Blowing five bucks of my own money to drag a lush out of the gutter was another way of looking at it. But I chose the former. I couldn't decide whether this was self-delusion or denial, two of my favorite pastimes. But it did take my mind off the irritating fact that I was missing *Gilligan's Island.*

When I arrived at The Flicker the streets were quiet. It was cold and the jet-set or the beautiful people or the Pepsi Generation or whatever they called themselves were either in the theaters or the bars. I found a place to park at the curb without risking a ticket. As a cab driver I could have parked in a loading zone and maybe gotten away with leaving my cab for a few minutes, but it was dicey. Cops generally give cabbies a lot of leeway, but they'll ticket an unoccupied taxi.

I grabbed the purse and got out and hurried to the front door of The Flicker. I was wearing only a T-shirt and blue jeans, as well as my deep forest green Rocky cap, and it seemed colder now than half an hour earlier. I once made a casual study of how much time I actually spent outside of my taxi during a single week, removing luggage or collecting fares, and it averaged 47 seconds per stop. Ergo, I always store my coat in the trunk.

The lobby of The Flicker was nice and warm and smelled like popcorn and champagne. Whenever they show *Night of the Living Dead* it smells different. The ticket booth was just an ordinary counter next to the candy stand. A young woman was seated behind the cash register toting her evening's take. I walked over and raised the purse. I pinched the brim of my cap like a cop flashing his badge, and told her that a fare had left her purse in my backseat and I needed to find her and give it back.

"I'm sorry," she said, "but the movie has started."

Okay. I've been around the block a few times in my taxi, and I served two years in the army, so I didn't need a translator to tell me where this was headed.

"Would it be all right if I just stepped into the auditorium for a minute and looked for her?" I said.

"I'm sorry, sir," she said. "But no one is allowed inside the theater after the movie has begun."

You have to understand. I love movies. The only thing I love more than movies is television. Flights of pure fantasy are not only important to me, they have helped me to avoid planning my future. But I have never bought into the idea that movies are sacred, barring the last ten minutes of *Psycho.* So when she said this to me, I felt like I was being conned by a used car salesman.

Maybe it was because I wasn't seated inside my taxicab, where I am in complete control of my universe, but suddenly I heard myself saying, "May I please speak to the manager?"

"He's running the projector," she said.

She continued counting the take from the cash register, and all of a sudden her face turned into Rollo's face. I realized that I was dealing with someone in complete control of her universe.

There's an old canard that I first heard in college, which goes like this: "What would happen if an irresistible force met an immovable object?" I learned the answer that night. The irresistible force loses. I know it sounds crazy but it's true. Don't ask me why—I didn't major in physics.

Throughout the entirety of this fruitless entreaty I felt my blood pressure rising. I'm not sure if it was because I was affronted by her religious adherence to a nonsensical rule, or because I wasn't getting my way. Perhaps a bit of both.

Since I had already lost the battle and I knew it, I decided there was only one thing to do: put my sarcasm on full-automatic and go down sneering.

"We are talking Robert Redford here, you know," I said.

One of her eyelashes batted.

I had drawn first blood.

"I mean I could understand if you were showing a Three Stooges marathon. But Bruce Dern? Karen Black? I could unleash a skunk in the theater and nobody would notice."

She took her eyes off the money and looked at me. Her face was getting red.

I smiled wanly and said, "You do realize that the script was written by Francis Ford Coppola."

She slapped her cash down and glared at me. "Nelson Riddle's score won an Oscar."

I took a hit, but it was a only a flesh wound.

I reached into my arsenal and pulled out my last big gun.

"Leonard Maltin gives it only one star."

She slammed the cash drawer shut and pursed her lips.

I waited hopefully for her to say, "Do you want me to go get the manager?" but instead she raised a finger and pointed at the wall behind her. "Do you see that sign?"

It was a cardboard recapitulation of the nonsensical rule. It cut me off at the knees. I had no defense to counter her move because the rule was written in ink. The printed word is sacred to me because I'm an unpublished novelist. But let's not get into that.

"What time does the movie let out?" I said.

She opened the cash drawer and picked up the bills and began counting them. "I would think that an aficionado of your caliber would already know the answer to that, Mister Show-Biz," she said.

In fact I knew exactly how long the movie was: 144 minutes. I knew this because I had sat through every single one of them when *The Great Gatsby* was in first-run. I decided to back off completely. Even losers know when to quit. It just takes them longer than winners.

I draped the purse over my arm and walked out the door. I figured the best thing to do would be to return to Rocky Cab and hand this albatross over to Rollo and go home and turn on my TV and forget that I ever heard of Bruce Dern.

Don't get me wrong though. I'm a big fan of Bruce Dern, as well as Karen Black. And I had long ago forgiven Robert Redford for making *Little Fauss and Big Halsy*. But that nonsensical rule had gotten my Irish up. Me and rules have never gotten along very well. That's probably why—correction—that's exactly why I was discharged from the army as a private. I didn't blame the cashier. She was just following orders. I'm sure I would have acted the same way if I had ever followed an order.

I climbed back into my hack, Rocky Mountain Taxicab #127, and looked at my wristwatch. It was evident that I would now be sacrificing ten dollars for having tried to save the flapper. I would never make it back to the motor before the second half-hour had begun. There was no use hanging around the theater waiting for the movie to end. I pulled away from the curb and headed back along the same route I had driven after I had dropped off Zelda.

I now realized that I should have just handed the purse over to Rollo, and forgotten about it. I had no business getting involved in any way in the personal life of one of my fares, a lesson I never seemed to learn over and over again. As I am fond of saying, sometimes you just have to do things before you realize how stupid they are.

By the way, just for your info, Leonard Maltin gives *The Great Gatsby* two-and-a-half stars. Now you know the ugly truth about me. When I fight bureaucracy, I fight dirty.

CHAPTER 3

Rollo was off duty by the time I got back. This came as a relief. I didn't mind being embarrassed in front of the night-shift cage man, an elderly, affable fellow who has been at Rocky Cab longer than me and who had been a driver in his youth. His name was Stew. He had driven a Checker Cab back when that company was still in the business of manufacturing the finest, most durable automobile ever built in the entire history of the human race. Tip: don't ever get Stew started on the glories of the Checker Cab versus the modern passenger vehicle. It's worse than listening to my Maw talk about the supremacy of radio over television.

I paid my ten-dollar late fee, was embarrassed for one minute, then walked out of the on-call room with the flapper's purse in my plastic briefcase. I had decided that I was going to return to The Flicker after the movie was over and see if I could find the girl. If that didn't work, I would ask one of the patrons where the after-movie party was being held so I could scout her out.

I know. You don't have to remind me. Getting involved in the personal lives of my fares is something that I vow never to do at least once a week. But I had no intention of getting involved in the flapper's personal problems, of which I was certain she had many, what with her being so young and drunk and irresponsible with money. I've been there. That was what made me decide to give it one last shot. I may not know much about almost everything, but I've been flat-busted in my lifetime and it's the lowest feeling in the world—next to losing my TV remote.

I climbed into my heap. My civilian car is a black 1964 Chevy with red doors. Why it has red doors is a long story. Remind me to tell it to you the next time we're in Sweeney's Tavern hiding from Stew. Word of advice: if the new bartender, Harold, is on duty at Sweeney's, don't say the word "run" in his presence. He'll invite you to join him for a mile run on the indoor track at the YMCA. You stand warned.

I drove back to my apartment on Capitol Hill where I live on the top floor of a three-story apartment building. I call it my "crow's nest." The reason I call it that is a long story, too, but I'll make it short. I can see the rooftops of the city from up there. Is that short enough?

I parked in the dirt lot behind my building and climbed the fire escape to the back door that leads into my kitchen. The kitchen is like a big box that was added on long before I came to Denver. The box extends a little ways out over the parking lot. It was added on by whoever converted the building into apartments. The building had been a private residence in the nineteenth century, back when Capitol Hill was where the millionaires lived before the Silver Boom went bust and everybody had to get real jobs. The Molly Brown House is located not far from where I live. You may have seen Molly Brown in the *The Unsinkable Molly Brown*. She was played by Debbie Reynolds.

Molly Brown was a poverty-stricken mountain girl who married a man named Horace Tabor who struck it rich with a silver mine. Apparently getting rich by working hard annoyed all the wealthy people, who had inherited their dough the way God intended, because they snubbed Molly who tried to elbow her way into Denver's high society. I personally try to avoid movies that use the words "Denver" and "high society" in the same plot, but I'm a sucker for Meredith Willson musicals. Plus, I'm always curious about a new take on the sinking of the *Titanic*. Okay. I'll admit it. I once thought of doing a coffee-table book about the different ways Hollywood has portrayed the sinking of the *Titanic*. That's probably why people like me are called "unpublished authors."

After I got inside my apartment I went to the bookshelf and withdrew my copy of *Finnegans Wake*. That's where I keep my taxi profits. I put the seventy bucks into the Shem and Shaun section, then turned on the TV just to have some noise. I went into the kitchen and fried a hamburger, and started thinking about writing. Specifically, I started thinking about writing a new screenplay.

I've been writing novels and screenplays for twenty years, and it looks like there's no end in sight. Part of it has to do with the fact that I earned a degree in English from the University of Colorado at Denver, although not on purpose. I went to school on the GI Bill only because Uncle Sam was willing to pay me three hundred bucks a month to do nothing, and I figured what the heck, I might as well put my army training to use.

When I first got drafted I had the sinking feeling in my gut that the Pentagon was going to make me do things, but my sergeants quickly divested me of that illusion—I didn't consider mopping floors to be doing anything, at least in terms of significant results. My sergeants seemed to agree with me there. Of course it all depended on your definition of "doing things." My concept of the army making me "do things" was directly related to the idea of performing activities that could conceivably kill another human being, such as being a cook.

But my inability in basic training to follow orders apparently had some bearing on my future job assignments, because at the end of basic I was sent to a private school. That's a school for draftees who are destined to remain privates.

After I got out of the army I had four years worth of GI Bill money available that I could use to go to college. Somehow I managed to stretch it out to seven years, probably because I was never very good at arithmetic. And since I wanted to continue doing nothing, I majored in English and subsequently got sidetracked into trying to become a novelist because my Maw once told me that novelists got paid to do what most people learned to do in grade school, which was to write sentences. I have since read a lot of how-to books trying to find out what the "trick" to writing novels is. It took me ten years to learn that the trick is getting paid.

I ate my hamburger and did the dish, then I went into my living room and opened the steamer trunk where I keep my vast collection of unpublished, unpublishable, and uncompleted novels, as well as unsold screenplays. I do have completed and uncompleted screenplays, but they both fall into the category of "unsold." I've seen quite a few movies where the screenplays seemed to be in the "uncompleted" category yet still got sold and made into movies, so I generally refer to all screenplays as "sold" or "unsold." But that's just my own filing system. I'm sure Hollywood has a simpler system.

It had been a year since I had completed an unsold screenplay. The arrival of the annual Mile-Hi International Film Festival always got my creative juices flowing, and the prospect of writing a one hundred and twenty page screenplay rather than a four hundred page novel was seductive. It made me feel as if I already had written two hundred and eighty pages of a novel and was in the home stretch before I had even typed FADE IN.

Another seductive aspect of screenwriting is that you're really only writing an outline. With a novel, you have to do an outline first and then write the book, but with a screenplay you just knock out the outline and sell it. I don't know why the publishers in New York don't take a tip from Hollywood and just publish the outlines of novels rather than the completed books. Let the audience use their imaginations, as my Maw always says about radio. I would much prefer to read an outline of *War and Peace* than slog through eight hundred thousand words. Why do I need Tolstoy to describe snow? I can imagine snow, whether Russian snow or just regular snow. But book publishers seem to think that the authors should do all the work, and the readers should be waited on hand-and-foot like a buncha goddamn prima donnas.

Ergo, the special appeal of screenwriting.

I had an hour left before I had to go back to The Flicker and start looking for the flapper, so I decided to try to kick-start a new screenplay by putting myself into the writing frame of mind. I have various techniques for doing this, and when it comes to concocting screenplays I sit in my easy chair and relax in silence for a minute, and then I switch on my TV and watch a movie. I do this with the sound off of course, since movies are stories told in pictures. The viewing of silent images reduces the creative process of filmmaking to its basic element. This allows me to absorb the director's vision unimpeded by sound effects, dialogue, or music. I can watch the forward progression of a story building to a climax through pure action, although sometimes I will switch channels so the movie is suddenly appended to another movie. For instance, Humphrey Bogart might be running down a dark alley with a drawn pistol and suddenly turn into a ballerina. This will get me laughing so hard that the extended dream will be broken and my desire to start writing a screenplay will be shattered beyond repair. I usually end up making my own movie out of TV commercials, sitcoms, and live broadcasts from zoos and wars.

This is also one of the peripheral rituals that prevents me from thinking about plots. I have a hard time with plots. Who the hell invented "plots" anyway? To me, a plot is just a cheap gimmick to keep people interested in a story.

But that night I became so absorbed in my remote screenwriting that I lost track of time. I suddenly glanced at my wristwatch and realized I had better get on the ball. The Great Gatsby himself would be laying face down in a swimming pool soon, and I wanted to get to the theater before Daisy's dock started flickering.

I closed up the writing workshop, turned off the TV, and left through the kitchen door. I climbed down the fire escape and before I got into my heap, I opened the trunk and pulled out my deep forest green Rocky Cab jacket and cap and put them on. I wanted to be wearing something vaguely official when I approached the girl to return her purse.

I drove back downtown with the purse lying beside me on the seat. It made me uneasy to be hauling all that cash, since it wasn't mine. I hadn't looked to see if the wad contained more than one Ben Franklin. It might have been wrapped around a wad of Washingtons for all I knew, but I didn't want to know. I just wanted to get rid of it.

Every time I passed a police car I felt guilty. Most people feel guilty whenever they see a cop car, since most people are usually "up to something." Whether it's Tom Edison or Jimmy Valentine, real Americans are always "up to something." That's part of what makes this country great. I'm the exception of course, since I'm never up to anything, which cops have a hard time believing when they pull me over. I think it's the red doors on my black Chevy. As many times as my Chevy has been stolen and then abandoned by thieves, you'd think the cops would be hip to my profile.

When I arrived at The Flicker, the sidewalks were deserted. Apparently nobody had left the theater yet. This surprised me, since I had walked out on *The Great Gatsby* three times before I finally sat all the way through it. My fourth date insisted on it.

CHAPTER 4

I positioned myself on the sidewalk so I would have a view of everyone passing through the doorway. The Flicker isn't a very large theater. The screen is small, though not mini-complex molecular. The audience started coming out. I expected the place to empty within five minutes. The crowd thickened, then thinned, but I didn't see the girl. I started to get irritated for a couple of reasons—primarily because my plan had seemed flawless and I had been certain that I would see her coming out the door, especially in that dazzling white dress. But I was also irritated because she may not, after all, have gone to see the movie. She might have met someone and gone somewhere else—not that she necessarily had lied to me, but her misinformation would have rendered my brilliant tactic moot, and my ego resented it.

Then people dressed like Zelda began coming past me from behind and I realized that The Flicker had a side exit that I had forgotten about. She might have come out the side door and walked away without my seeing her. My ego took another flesh wound. My scheme fell apart before my eyes. There was only one thing to do.

I tugged my Rocky cap low, adjusted my collar, and walked toward two dolls decked out in sequins and feathers and asked them where the after-movie party was. They looked me up and down and kept walking. I'm fairly used to that, so I approached a dapper guy in tails and asked him for directions. He told me the party was being held in a converted warehouse in LoDo.

LoDo is an abbreviation for Lower Downtown Denver, the part of town near Union Station at the edge of the valley where the Platte River flows. People in Denver like to say "LoDo." It makes them feel "in with the in-crowd." I know because that's how it makes me feel. During the nineteenth century, LoDo was basically the central part of downtown. Prior to being warehouses, many of the buildings were whorehouses. A madame named Mattie Silks ran a crib down on Market Street, which originally was called Holladay Street, but the rich Holladay family got the City Council to change the name to "Market Street" because they didn't want their name associated with soiled doves. I know quite a bit about whorehouses. I took a Denver history class at UCD. I swear that's the actual reason.

I thanked the dapper chap and went back to my heap and got in. I headed down Larimer and circled around to Blake Street and followed it for a few blocks. The old warehouse was near Blake and 16th. It was a four-story red brick building that had been turned into an art gallery. I knew the place. I had dropped people off there before but I had never been inside. I have never been inside almost every place I ever dropped people off, which leads me to believe that there's something slightly superficial about cab driving.

I parked at the curb, got out and zipped my jacket to the neck. It was damn cold out by now. I hoped that the flapper had gotten hold of some kind of coat, although vodka makes pretty good insulation. The party people were arriving in cars and on foot, many of them from the direction of The Flicker, which was within walking distance. I could have walked to the place, too, but there's a lot of things in this world I could do that I don't. A band was playing inside the warehouse. Jazz-age music, Charleston brass, horns, and drums. It sounded like fun, but I've got my own ideas about fun, and they do not involve standing up.

I followed a small group of laughing couples through the doorway into a lighted foyer. It was warm in there. It smelled of champagne and rotting wood. The place was at least a hundred years old. I paused in the foyer and let a few more couples pass by. There was a phone in one corner of the foyer. A kid wearing a raccoon coat and a straw boater was hunched around it talking into the receiver. He was wearing black-framed glasses. He looked like Harold Lloyd. I liked that.

A man wearing a tuxedo and top hat was standing at the door that led into the dancehall. As I approached the entrance he gave me "the eye" and said, "Do you have an invitation?"

I pinched the bill of my cap and told him that I wasn't there for the party, that I was looking for a fare I had dropped off.

He looked my Rocky Cab costume up and down and said, "I'm sorry, but I can't let you into the hall without an invitation."

I reached into my jacket pocket and pulled out the purse.

"She left this in the backseat of my taxi," I said. "I just want to return it to her. If you'll let me go inside and look around, I'll be out in a couple of minutes."

"I'm sorry," he said, "but I can't do that."

"Why not?"

"Because you're not dressed properly."

"I'm a cab driver," I said. "Cab drivers never dress properly."

"This is a nostalgia party," the guy said. "If you come back dressed like a cabbie from the 1920s, I can let you in."

For a moment I considered muscling my way past the gold-hatted high-bouncer and crashing the party, but I didn't want to ruin everybody's fun. I do enough of that when my friends throw parties.

Instead I turned and walked back toward the exit, accepting the fact that there are times in my life when I simply will not get my way, as rare as they are.

"Fine! Who cares? To hell with you!"

I froze.

Was I talking out loud again?

I looked around just as the kid in the raccoon coat slammed the phone down on the cradle. He was the hard case in this foyer.

He glanced at me from behind those thick-framed glasses. He looked like an infuriated Harold Lloyd. I liked that even better. When he realized I was looking at him, he glanced away in embarrassment. Then he looked back at me and said, "Are you really a cab driver?"

Five minutes later I looked just like Harold Lloyd.

I walked up to the gatekeeper and handed him an engraved invitation.

"I saw you do that," he said.

"Your point being ... ?" I replied.

He shrugged, took the invitation, and stood back to let me into the world of the Roaring Twenties, of gangsters and prohibition, of gin and jazz, of the beautiful and the damned. A band was playing at the far end of the room, young musicians in red-and-white pinstriped outfits on a bandstand lit with colored spots. A glitter-ball hung from the ceiling sending a shower of light spinning across the faces of the damned. Already I was getting overheated and it wasn't the floozies in their tight flapper skirts. It was the raccoon coat that I had borrowed from the angry kid in the foyer.

He had arrived at this orgy expecting his girlfriend to meet him here, but she didn't show. Ergo, the angry phone call. He had decided to split, and that's why he asked me if I was a cab driver. I did some fast talking, and we cut a deal.

I edged around the room. It looked like someone had torn out all the walls that made up the original cubicles of this place. It also looked like the second floor had been removed. It was high-ceilinged and hollow. It was a good place to put a ballroom. Only one thing bothered me. The wooden floor seemed to be bouncing a bit. But I ignored this and made my way around the edge of the dance floor, looking for a white dress. There were a lot of bodies doing the Charleston in the middle of the bouncing floor. I didn't like the look of that bounce. This place wasn't built for dancing. That made two of us.

I completed the circuit of the room and still didn't see the girl. Already I was beginning to accept the utter futility of my mission. I decided to move into the crowd rather than skirt the edges. I pulled the straw hat down tight against my head and adjusted the Harold Lloyd glasses. Suddenly I saw someone I recognized. Two someones. They were the dolls who had snubbed me back at The Flicker. They were holding drinks and swiveling their heads this way and that, taking in the scene. They saw me in my raccoon coat and their faces lit up. "You're the mosquitoes knuckles!" one of them said. I looked her up and down and kept on walking.

This was the first time I had ever worn a rented costume, and the anonymity seemed to set me free. I no longer felt like I was me, so you can imagine what a thrill it was. I would highly recommend a rental costume to anybody consumed with self-loathing. It has to be cheaper than a psychiatrist.

I made the circuit of the crowd, then gave it up. I couldn't find the girl, and I'm pretty good at finding girls. I knew it was time to throw in the towel. I glanced at my wristwatch. It was ten o'clock, my usual time for giving up. I turned back toward the exit and edged through the crowd until I emerged into the foyer of the real world. I didn't especially want to be in the real world, but that's where my car was.

The kid was leaning against the wall by the door, my hat in his hand. He glanced at me as I exited the ballroom. "Did you find her?" he said. He knew about the purse. I shook my head no, and he shook his head with understanding. It was "the night of the missing girls."

We exchanged costumes. We stepped outside into the cold. I had told him during the closing of The Deal that I was off-duty, but that I had my own car. He had agreed to let me give him a free ride home in exchange for the use of his threads.

As we walked away I kept thinking about that bouncing floor. It was like a wooden trampoline. It seemed unsafe. The building was ancient. But I figured the only thing I could do about it was check the headlines in the morning papers.

He got in shotgun. When I drive cab #127 I try to keep people from sitting shotgun, and not necessarily for safety reasons, which is one of the official reasons for keeping a fare out of the front seat. I do this by cluttering the shotgun seat with my plastic briefcase, paperback books, empty Coke cans, and empty Twinkie wrappers. It generally works, unless the fare happens to be another taxi driver. For some reason taxi drivers feel they have a right to sit shotgun in a cab. I suppose it makes them feel "in with the in-crowd." I never sit shotgun when I ride in a taxi, which I usually do from Sweeney's or anybody else's tavern. And I never tell another taxi driver that I'm a taxi driver. I usually call Yellow Cab or Metro Taxi, I rarely call Rocky Cab for a ride. I do this because I like riding incognito. I ask the drivers inane questions about cab driving: what's it like, how much money do you make, is it dangerous, do you ever have weird experiences? It's a "game" I play, although I assume psychiatrists have a technical term for it.

But since this was an unofficial cab ride, I didn't mind the guy sitting in the front seat. As we drove down Blake Street I told him about my car being stolen every now and then from my apartment building on Capitol Hill, and how the vermin who had taken it a few years back had ripped off my doors. I had replaced them with doors that I had found in a junkyard. Red was the only color I could find. Now you know the story, too. We'll have to talk about something else the next time we're hiding out from Stew.

CHAPTER 5

I dropped the guy off on Federal Boulevard, then headed north until I
came to the I-70 interchange. It would be a fast trip to Rocky on the
interstate, for which I was grateful because I wanted to get home and start
forgetting. I usually do that by seven-thirty. I was way behind schedule.

As I drove along the highway I started thinking about a saying I used
to hear at Dyna-Plex, the company in the Denver Tech Center where I
used to work: "No good deed shall go unpunished." The executives at
Dyna-Plex were fond of saying this. They were fond of saying a lot of
things that amounted to corporate aphorisms, like "reinvent the wheel"
and "work smarter, not harder," and "think outside the box." But again,
the one I liked best and thought about long after I had left the company
was "no good deed shall go unpunished." I had never thought of corporate America as a bastion of profound philosophical thought, but I
couldn't think of anything nice I had ever done for anybody that didn't
turn into a disaster, alienate my friends, or put my life in jeopardy, often
at the same time.

It's true that I was motivated by the potential of scoring a big tip
from a young woman who carried a hundred-dollar bill in her purse, but
I would have done this even without that motive. I've been known to do
lots of things that hold no promise whatsoever of personal profit, such as
writing novels.

I parked my car in a rank of taxis and got out. It felt strange to be at
Rocky so late at night and off duty. It reminded me of a dream I sometimes have where I come to the cab company and take a taxi without
authorization and drive around Denver illegally. It makes me wonder if

I might have done something similar to that in a previous lifetime—like the army. I drank a lot of beer in the army.

I went into the on-call room, which was quiet. There were a couple of cabbies hanging around waiting for their vehicles to come in from the road. I walked up to the cage where Stew was seated eating a sandwich and listening to a portable radio. He was listening to an oldies station. Andrews Sisters oldies. I pulled the purse out of my pocket and set it on the counter.

"A fare left this in my cab this evening," I said.

Stew set his sandwich down, pulled a pair of glasses out of his shirt pocket, and went through the process of attaching them to his face. He raised his chin and peered down his nose at the purse with his mouth slightly parted, the way old men do. I've never seen a child do this. I sometimes think old men are faking it.

"What time was this?" he said.

"Around six-thirty this evening," I said.

He frowned at me, so I explained the business about trying to track down the flapper.

He frowned deeper and said, "You shouldn't have done that, Murph. You should have turned the purse in before you signed out."

I told him I knew that, but I figured I could find the girl since I knew she was at The Flicker—or I thought she was there. "But when I didn't find her I went to this party where I thought she might be, but I didn't find her there either."

Stew listened to this recital with slitted eyes. The punishment had begun.

"Anyway, there's some money in the purse," I said, "so I figured I better bring it back tonight."

His frown got deeper, almost as deep as a frown I once saw on a security guard at a dog track, but that's another story.

Stew picked up the purse and slowly opened it and looked inside. He gave a low whistle, then raised his head and looked at two men seated at a table waiting for their cabs.

"Lewis. Nagle. Come here," he said.

They looked at him warily, then gave me "the eye." I knew what they were thinking—Murph has gotten us involved in some kind of mess. I had the feeling I was about to alienate some more friends.

Lewis and Nagle got up and lethargically strolled over to the cage.

"I need you guys to be witnesses," Stew said. "I have to count out some money here."

I glanced quickly at what I now knew were my ex-friends, and just as quickly looked away.

Stew pulled the wad of money out of the purse and unrolled it. The entire stack was made up of Ben Franklins. Three of the men whistled. The fourth one didn't. That was me. I have a hard time whistling in the presence of my enemies.

Stew counted out the money. It came to twelve hundred dollars. Each of us was asked to count the money personally while the others watched. Then Stew made us sign a paper that he drew up, a kind of receipt that showed how much money was found in the purse, what time it was turned in, and who witnessed it. The receipt would be turned in to Hogan, the Rocky Cab supervising manager. Stew placed the purse inside a paper bag and stapled it closed.

The procedure was clean. All the legalities were taken care of. All the tees were crossed and all the eyes were dotted. The only question that remained was whether I would get out of the parking lot alive.

I thought about hiding in the men's room until Lewis and Nagle went on duty, but I didn't know how long that would take. I finally said something about how invigorated I felt after my kung-fu class that evening. After I got out the door I ran to my heap. Thank God Lewis and Nagle were night drivers. With any luck, I would never see them again as long as I lived, assuming I never pulled another night shift, and like I always say, "Now is as good a time as any to start not doing things."

CHAPTER 6

I slept well that night. I had Tuesday off, I was going to a film festival, and I had gotten rid of an albatross. I rolled out of the sack at ten and decided to add to the specialness of the day by cooking fried eggs instead of a hamburger. After the eggs were done I slipped them between the layers of a hamburger bun and carried it with a can of Coke into the living room and switched on my TV. I popped open the Coke and took my first snort of the day. Bachelor breakfast.

It was a little early for *Gilligan's Island.* Not that Gilligan wasn't showing, but watching Mary Ann strut around the island in her denim short-shorts at that moment would have been like drinking before noon, which I abandoned after I got out of the army.

I settled on garden-variety channel surfing as I broke my fast, checking out the wars and zoos. When my eggburger was gone, I shut off the TV and pulled out the Mile-Hi Film Festival schedule in order to re-check all the movies I didn't want to see. There were a lot of them. Most of the ones I didn't want to see had been made by "promising young directors." I figured I would wait until they had come through on a few of their promises before I started shoving money into their pockets.

The festival was featuring a number of retrospectives by directors who had come through on their promises, as well as a mixture of student films, low-budget independent films, and just plain bad movies made by people from all over the United States who had no money.

I generally try to avoid paying attention to the plot in a feature-length film, especially if the film was made by a "promising young director," but that's usually no problem in short subjects which are anecdotal in nature and you're lucky if they have a point to them much less a plot—sort of like *New Yorker* stories but not as difficult to sit through. It took me years to realize that the difference between novels and movies is that people will watch anything that moves, whereas reading takes a certain amount of effort. By "certain" I mean "minimal," which may explain why I read more than I work. If it moves though, I'll watch it.

The short-subject program was scheduled for two in the afternoon at the Ogden Theater. There was another program I wanted to catch at five P.M., an international cartoon showcase. This was always a popular venue at the festival, and the theater would probably be packed. It was playing at the Vogue Theater down on south Pearl Street, which would give me an hour to get there and find a good seat. If I had planned to drive my heap I wouldn't have any nick-of-time problem, but I would be riding in a taxi because I intended to make a stop at the Starlight Lounge before going to the first program. Beer helps me to not concentrate on the plot if a film happens to have one.

I decided to call Yellow Cab for my trip to the Ogden Theater. The Ogden is not that far away from where I live, so I could have walked, but we've had that conversation.

I was waiting in front of my apartment when the Yellow pulled up at the curb. I didn't recognize the driver. Sometimes I do. I know a lot of drivers from the other cab companies since I encounter them when I'm waiting outside the hotels. But unlike a lot of cabbies, I don't stand around outside my taxi and shoot the breeze while waiting for fares. I know less about sports than I do about the meaning of existence, which seems to be the two subjects the drivers like to discuss, so I'm kind of a wet blanket. I just sit in my cab and read paperbacks and hope none of the drivers knock on my window and try to sell me homemade jewelry.

I climbed into the backseat of the Yellow and shut the door and told the driver I was going to the Ogden Theater, but first I needed to stop at a 7-11 store and get some money from an ATM machine. I knew the driver would be pissed at having a three-dollar trip, so I wanted to give him at least five dollars plus a tip without looking like the softie that I am. But I also wanted to buy candy bars and a Twinkie to smuggle into the Ogden. I was wearing my "big" coat. Goose down. Colorado camouflage. I could have told the driver I was buying snacks for the movie but I never like people knowing what I'm up to. On top of that, saying "ATM machine" made me feel important.

"So how's your day been?" I said as we pulled away from the curb. I was going into my "passenger" act.

"Pretty good," he replied.

"Making any money off the film festival?"

"Nah."

"Been driving long?"

"Six years."

"Do you like it?"

"Yeah."

"Do you start work in the morning or afternoon?"

"Afternoon. I just now came on duty."

"So I'm your first fare of the day?"

"Yeah."

"A friend of mine drives for Rocky Cab," I said. "He makes about fifty bucks a day. Do you make that much?"

"I make a hundred-twenty a day."

"Profit?"

"Yeah."

"Every day?"

"Yeah."

"I guess Yellow gets more calls than Rocky, huh?"

"Yeah. We're the best company."

"That's why I called you guys."

"Smart move."

"I notice you have a computer in your cab. The Rocky cabs don't have computers. Is that why you make more money?"

"Computers ain't got nothing to do with it. It's experience that counts."

By this time we were at the 7-11. I hopped out and went inside. A hundred-twenty profit my ass. I love cross-examining the competition. I bought three candy bars and a Twinkie. I was in college when I learned that chocolate goes well with beer, but that might be subjective. I went back outside and climbed into the Yellow.

"Are you going to any of the film festival movies this week?" I said as he pulled onto Colfax.

"Nah."

"Don't you like movies?"

"Ain't got time for movies."

"Do you work twelve-hour shifts?"

"Nah. I work eight hours a day."

"And you take home a hundred-twenty every day?"

"Yeah."

"On top of your lease payment and gas?"

"Yeah."

"You must rake in two hundred a day."

"Yeah."

"I was thinking of getting a job as a cab driver," I said. "I was going to apply at Rocky like my friend, but maybe I should work for Yellow."

"You'll make more money," he said.

"My friend works twelve-hour shifts and makes fifty bucks," I said.

"That's because he doesn't know what he's doing. You gotta know what you're doing."

He pulled up across the street from the Ogden Theater. The fare came to four-fifty and I gave him six bucks. "Have a nice day," I chirped as I climbed out. One hundred and ninety-four bucks to go, pal. Knock yourself out.

I looked up at the marquee. "Short-Subject Showcase 2 PM Be There" it said.

I'll be there, I mumbled. I'm used to taking orders from signs. I walked down the block to the Starlight Lounge. I always hit the Starlight before going to the Ogden, although usually at night. I stepped inside and took a seat on a padded stool. I didn't know the day-shift bartender so I didn't make any small talk. Drinking beer in the daytime is unusual for me—unless it's a weekend or a Tuesday or a Thursday. I usually drink only in my crow's nest. They never show *Gilligan's Island* at the Ogden.

I kept glancing at my watch as I drank my beers. Whenever I drink at the Starlight before going to a movie I become a time master. It's sort of like being a quarterback working the clock during the last two minutes of a football game. I do this when I'm driving too—not drinking beer, but working the clock. I never drink beer when I'm driving a cab. But when you're driving a cab and it's getting close to the end of the day, you sometimes have to make judgments about whether you have time to pick up one last fare before quitting. Making judgments normally irritates me, but when money is involved I don't mind so much. It's interesting to make judgments once in awhile. I should do that more often.

I managed to drink three beers before it was time to walk the half block to the Ogden. I could have squeezed in a fourth beer but I've seen too many Bronco quarterbacks make that mistake. I left a tip on the bar and walked out feeling pretty good. I was in the mood for bad filmmaking.

I bought a ticket and picked up a program in the lobby, then purchased a small Coke at the snack stand. I always buy a Coke as a penance for my Twinkies. I went up to the balcony and sat in the front row. The theater was only half full. Maybe there weren't that many short-subject fans in Denver, but then again maybe most Denverites were at work. The motion-picture industry must have been hit pretty hard when the Great Depression ended.

While I waited for the curtain to rise, I glanced at the program. I didn't read it too closely because I don't like to know what I'm in for when it comes to movies. Even though I don't consider movies sacred, I do believe in the sacredness of ignorance, and I don't want anybody telling me the plot, the funny parts, or the denouement of any film. A lot of human beings seem to have a deeply rooted psychological need to ruin movies for everybody else. I call it "The Rosebud Syndrome." This is when people tell you what "Rosebud" means so you won't have endure all that awful suspense. If you don't know what I'm talking about, consider yourself lucky.

I checked the program just to find out how many shows I would get to sit through: eight films in ninety minutes. Not bad. The most interesting title was a local production. It was called *The Man Who Crawled Across Denver*. The theater manager had saved it for the last reel, the bastard. I hate slick marketing.

I set the program aside and looked around. The Ogden balcony wasn't like it used to be in the old days before the government outlawed smoking practically everywhere. There was a time, twenty years back, when you could come to an avant-garde movie and the smoke in the balcony would be so thick you didn't even have to bring your own pot. I came here one night and saw *Eraserhead* three times before the curtain even rose.

The lights finally went down. I'm not going to tell you what the first seven films were about because, to my knowledge, I don't have any deeply rooted psychological needs. I gave them seven thumbs-up. But I'm going to tell you about *The Man Who Crawled Across Denver* because I guarantee that you will never see this movie anywhere. I won't be giving anything away, especially the plot. The title pretty much says it all.

It was about this guy who got down on his hands and knees on a sidewalk at what I judged to be the intersection of Colfax and York, and started crawling west. He passed a lot of people but nobody paid any attention to him. There was a smattering of applause in the audience when he crawled past the Ogden Theater. He took a few detours and crawled past places like the D&F Tower and Union Station and other local landmarks. I couldn't tell if the filmmaker intended that the audience believe he was crawling in a straight line, which he could not have done if he had crawled past those places, but I wrote that off as artistic license, i.e., show-biz. The man finally made it to west Colfax and Federal where he stood up.

The End.

I was particularly pleased by the fact that the movie made no sense. When I walked out of the Ogden I felt like a new man.

I called from a phone booth for a Metro Taxi. I had about an hour to go before the cartoon festival started at the Vogue but I wanted to get there with plenty of time to spare. There's a lot of nice little bars near the Vogue.

On the ride down to south Pearl Street I asked the Metro driver the same questions I had asked the Yellow driver. This guy claimed to net ninety bucks a day for a twelve-hour shift, which was plausible. The only reason I make fifty bucks a day when I drive is because I'm lazy. If I wanted to work hard I wouldn't be driving a taxi. I spent five years working hard before I discovered cab driving. Of course, my definition of "working hard" is anything that involves effort. But as Willie Sutton once said, "That's where the money is."

I made it to the Vogue with forty-five minutes to go. I downed two beers in a nearby joint before I made my way to the box office. The Vogue is a quaint venue located in a residential neighborhood. The theater is small, boxlike, and has a 1920s feel about it.

I'm not going to describe the cartoons I saw that night, save to say that they were worth the wait, like "The Best Of" TV commercials that come on the tube every now and then. You've probably been to a few animation festivals in your time—a lot of European stuff, avant-garde artwork, surreal sex, the whole shooting match.

The Vogue is like the Ogden in the sense that people don't smoke in there like they did in the old days. There's no balcony in the Vogue, but in the old days you didn't need a balcony to get high. There were a lot of kids in the audience that night, college-age, which is a part of what I like about going to cartoon festivals—being surrounded by young people who give me the delusion that I'm hip.

When the last animation ground to its existential halt and the lights came up, I followed the throng up the aisle and out to the street. I walked to a phone booth on the corner and called Rocky Cab for a ride home. I'd had my fill of chicanery for one day. Two hours of soul-satisfying animation had drained me of the hankering to secretly razz the competition. I just wanted to kick back and relax to the ticking sound of a meter transferring money from one Rocky Cab driver to another. I call this the Trickle Sideways Theory of getting nowhere fast.

CHAPTER 7

I woke up on Wednesday morning feeling invigorated. I made another eggburger before setting out for Rocky Cab. I stood eating it and sipping a Coke and looking out the kitchen window at clouds moving over the city. Snow clouds. I had mixed feelings. We cabbies refer to snow as "white gold." The radios in our taxis start hopping when snow starts falling because people hate to drive in the snow. I'm talking Colorado people. Don't ask me to explain that, although the influx of Californians during the past few years might. I myself hail from Wichita, Kansas, where the air is humid and the snow is wet. Denver has dry snow. I love science.

I thought about not driving that day because I hate driving when normal people are afraid to drive—it makes me feel like the wrong kind of outsider. But the odds were good that I would score a hundred bucks profit without even trying. It's a funny thing about a sure score. It makes me lethargic. The challenge disappears. I stood there chewing my eggburger and just staring out the window, feeling as if the money was already in my pocket and there was no reason to get a move on. It was the same feeling I had in college when I started writing my first novel. The feeling disappeared when I received my first rejection slip.

I closed my crow's nest and climbed down the fire escape, and already tiny flakes were tickling my face. I fired up my heap and headed for Rocky Cab. I had to turn on the windshield wipers before I got halfway there. This was going to be one of "those" snows, I could sense it. By the time I got to Rocky, the flakes had become big enough to recognize two of a kind.

The on-call room was packed with a few newbies as well as a lot of white-gold sourdoughs who would even go to work on a Saturday just to get in on the mother lode. When the radio is jumping and the old pros are working the asphalt, the newbies don't stand a chance. You don't just stroll into the Yukon and start picking up nuggets off the permafrost. You have to know your Jack London inside and out, and newbies don't know jack about snow driving. I felt sorry for them, just as I had felt sorry for myself back when I was a newbie.

I paid for my daily lease and picked up the key and trip-sheet for 127 from Rollo, who was too busy to even eat donuts. When I got outside the big flakes were coming down steadily. A night driver had just brought 127 in, so the cab was warmed up for me. That's always pleasant on a day like this. It added to my lethargy. I checked the oil and water, and looked for new dents on the body, which you always have to do or you get blamed for it—like everything else in life.

I drove to a 7-11 and gassed up and bought a Coke and Twinkie, then headed for downtown Denver listening to the radio, which was already jumping. I wanted to sit in front of a hotel while I ate brunch and see if I might score an airport run before diving into the gold fields. The line at the Brown Palace Hotel was short, so I barely had time to finish my Twinkie before a businessman came out wearing an overcoat and carrying a briefcase. "DIA," I said to myself. I was feeling both lethargic and smug. The man climbed into the backseat and said, "The history museum."

That burst my lethargic balloon. The Denver Museum of Natural History is on the east side of City Park. It's a six-dollar fare at best, maybe seven with a tip. But I didn't mind so much. Money is money, and this trip would thrust me into the gold fields. I knew I would be jumping bells after I dropped him off. That's cabbie lingo for radio calls from headquarters. I pulled away from the hotel and circled around and got onto 17th Avenue and headed for Colorado Boulevard, which runs adjacent to City Park. I made small talk. The man said he was in charge of a new exhibit that was being brought in from Taiwan. Something to do with statues made of jade. I pretended to be interested, which I had been good at since first grade.

After he got out of my cab, I paused in front of the museum and filled out my trip-sheet while listening for bells on that side of town. I didn't hear anything I liked. This is part of the smugness and lethargy and general cocksureness of driving on a day when half the city is desperate for cabs. I could have made a bundle just working the grocery stores, but that would have entailed loading my trunk with white plastic bags while standing in the snow, and then helping my fares carry the bags into their houses. Need I say more?

I drove out of the parking lot and made a right turn onto Colorado Boulevard and headed down toward 17th, and then reality came a-knocking. I tried to pull over into the center lane, but the steering wheel would not obey. I had hit black ice. It was hidden beneath a layer of snow. My wheels were no longer connected to the asphalt.

My lethargy abandoned ship. Adrenaline grabbed the tiller.

One hundred feet ahead of me stood a line of cars waiting for the red light on 17th, and I was sliding right toward them. My driver's ed teacher began screaming at me. I tapped the brakes but nothing happened. I kept sliding. I was seventy feet away from the rear-end of a Ford station wagon. I glanced in my rear-view mirror and saw a bus fifty feet behind me, but he was slowing down. Time was slowing down. Everything was slowing down but me. My heart was pounding. The front end of 127 drifted left. I turned the steering wheel to the right, but it was mutiny. I tapped the brakes. Nothing. I was fifty feet away from the Ford. I tapped and steered, and the front end began to drift right. I was thirty feet away from having the very first traffic accident of my cab-driving career, and I knew it. I felt sorry for the driver in the Ford. It was a woman with big hair. She was about to be introduced to me the hard way.

I looked in the rear-view mirror. The bus had stopped completely. So had the automobiles next to it. Everyone was watching the Rocky Cab swerving down Colorado Boulevard. I was their dog-and-pony show for the morning, something to talk about around the water cooler.

And then it happened.

The red light up ahead turned green and the cars in front of me started moving forward. I was twenty feet away from the Ford, but I stayed twenty feet away. The Ford was now moving at the same speed as I was sliding. Relativity had kicked in. Volition and chaos were indistinguishable. I love physics. The traffic ahead of me was pulling away. My cab slid over to the right side of the road and bounced against the curb. I let the wheels do the braking, rubbing against the curb. I looked in my mirror. The bus and its pals were still stopped, waiting for the smashing climax of this action adventure, but I had let them down. My cab came to a grinding halt.

I sat there gripping the steering wheel and listening to Gene Krupa on the aorta. My engine was dead. City Park was bathed in silence. I looked in the mirror at the swirls and sweeps of my tire tracks. The traffic light turned back to red. I reached down and grabbed the key and started the engine, put the shift into drive, and eased away from the curb. I crept to the intersection, then turned right and crept along the south side of City Park. It was a sign from God. I recognized it. He was telling me to get new tires.

I turned off both the Rocky radio and the AM radio to avoid any distractions, and I took it slow on the way back to the motor—cabbie lingo for headquarters. Black ice is one of the few things in life you can't argue with. That and nuns. I followed as many side streets as possible where the snow was still thick. When I got back to Rocky Cab I found a half-dozen other drivers who were complaining to Rollo that their tires weren't holding the road. Apparently the maintenance crew hadn't been keeping up with the demand for tires that performed well on ice.

I waited until the complainers had cleared out before I went up to the cage to let Rollo know I was back. I dislike complainers. As loyal as I am to the league of asphalt warriors, I have to admit that a lot of cabbies live to find something to bitch about, as if they are eager to share some of their perfection with the rest of the world. But having been yelled at by most of my employers ever since I got my first and only paper route, I have no delusions about the shabby state of my own perfection.

Rollo was scribbling notes with one hand and holding the inter-office phone in the other as I came up to the window.

"I need new tires," I said politely. I spoke to him the way I want people to speak to me—as little as possible.

He glanced up with a harried look. I liked that. Rollo rarely looks harried. He is in complete control of his universe, when the weather is nice.

"Murph! Where the hell have you been?" he said

Red flags started popping up all over my own universe.

"I've been trying to get back to the motor," I said. "My tires won't hold the ice."

"We've been trying to get you on the radio!" he said, slamming the phone down.

"What for?" I said.

"Hogan wants to see you in his office right away!"

"What about?"

I could see it in his eyes. He wanted to tell me, wanted to squeal, wanted to spill the beans, but he couldn't. Probably on orders from Hogan.

"It's serious," his eyes said, but his mouth remained shut. In my line of work, and in my rear-view mirror, you see a lot of eyes. I know my eyes.

His mouth started talking. "You'd better get up there," it said. But Rollo didn't seem to be taking any pleasure in this. I wondered if he was well. He usually smiles with malicious condescension whenever Hogan calls me on the carpet.

"My taxi needs new tires," I said. "Can you have the mechanics take care of that while I'm upstairs?"

I waited for Rollo to say something sarcastic, to give me some grief, to reply with malicious condescension. I wanted things to be normal. But he just nodded.

I crossed the room, entered the hallway, and climbed the stairs that led to the managing supervisor's office. The door at the top of the stairs was closed. I knocked.

"Come in," Hogan said. This surprised me. He usually just says "Yeah" as if he'd rather say "Nah."

I opened the door and stepped into his office, and saw two men wearing suits. They were seated in chairs by Hogan's desk. They looked like plainclothes cops. I know what plainclothes cops look like. I watch a lot of TV.

"Thanks for coming in, Murph," Hogan said. "We had a little trouble getting hold of you on the radio."

"I had my radio off," I said.

The suits glanced at each other. They both stood up from their chairs.

"Have a seat, Murph," Hogan said.

I sat down uneasily. I hadn't sat in one of Hogan's chairs since the day I applied for this job.

"We've got a little problem here," Hogan said. "This is Detective Duncan and Detective Argyle from the Denver Police Department. They want to ask you a few questions. Is that all right with you?"

I nodded, then I remembered to smile, then I remembered to speak. "Sure," I said.

"Do you always drive around with your radio off?" Detective Duncan said.

He was standing right next to my chair. I looked up at him. "Yes."

He frowned.

I didn't think that was the answer he was looking for.

"Isn't that how you get your fares?" he said.

I shrugged. "I work the hotels a lot. I don't jump bells unless I have to."

"Jump bells?" Detective Argyle said.

"Take calls off the radio," I said, looking over at him. "When I'm waiting outside a hotel I don't keep my radio on. I read paperback books."

"Is that standard operating procedure at this taxi company?" Duncan said. I looked up at him. He was looking at Hogan.

"We advise the drivers to keep their radios on at all times for safety's sake," Hogan said. "But there's no hard and fast rule. The drivers are independent operators. We leave it up to them."

"If your radio was off, how did you know to come back just now and talk to Mr. Hogan?" Duncan said.

"I didn't," I said.

The cops glanced at each other.

"Then why are you here?" Duncan said.

I began to get the funny feeling that I was being evasive. So I explained about my near-accident on Colorado Boulevard, and how I had come back to get new tires.

Hogan spoke to the cops. "We've got a lot of drivers downstairs who came back to have new tires put on their taxis," he said.

They nodded. Then Duncan came around in front of my chair and looked down at me. "Did you pick up a fare on east Fourteenth Avenue Monday night?"

I nodded. I gave him the address.

He reached for a trip-sheet on Hogan's desk and held it up for me to see. It was my Monday trip-sheet. He pointed at the last entry. "Did you fill this out yourself?"

"Yes."

"Who did you pick up at this address?"

"A young lady. She had been drinking."

"Where did you take her?"

"To The Flicker. It's a movie theater on Larimer Square."

"How was she dressed?"

"Like Zelda Fitzgerald."

Argyle picked up a paper bag that was lying on Hogan's desk. He reached in and pulled out a white purse.

"Is this her purse?"

I stared at it. Then I nodded and started to close my eyes, resigning myself to the fact that the good deed was going where all good deeds must go. But I quickly realized that eye-closing would be tantamount to confessing to a crime I hadn't committed. I had seen *In Cold Blood* twice, the feature film and the made-for-TV movie. Why they remade that movie I will never understand.

CHAPTER 8

I braked my eyelids and looked up at Duncan. "I don't know for a fact that it's her purse, but I assumed it was when I turned it in to the lost-and-found."

"You assumed?"

"Yes."

"Why did you assume that?"

"Because it looked just like the purse she was carrying when she got into my cab."

Argyle set the purse on the desk next to me.

"According to our report, you dropped the lady off at the movie theater around six forty-five. You were due to turn your taxi in at seven o'clock, yet you didn't turn it in until almost eight o'clock. And you didn't turn the purse in until ten o'clock that night."

He stopped talking. A silence filled the room. I began to get the feeling that I needed a lawyer. I wondered if E.G. Marshall was available.

"Can you explain the time discrepancies?" Argyle said.

As you might surmise, I was starting to get rattled. Two detectives. A purse filled with money. A drunken flapper. A driver who looked like me. Do I have to paint you a picture?

"I got back here at seven," I said. "I was cleaning up my cab when I found the purse. So I decided to go back to The Flicker and return it. I figured she would need it."

"Did you open the purse?"

"Yes."

"What did you find inside it?"

"A tube of lipstick and some money."

"How much money?"

"I couldn't tell right then. I didn't find out until later. It was sort of rolled up. There was a one-hundred-dollar bill on the outside. I closed the purse and decided to take it back to her."

The cops glanced at each other.

"So you came here at seven, and then left again?" Duncan said.

"Yes."

"And you got back at eight?"

"Yes."

"Why didn't you turn the purse in at eight?" Duncan said.

"What did you do between eight and ten?" Argyle said.

I looked from one to the other, trying to decide who to answer. Then I realized they were playing bad-cop/bad-cop.

I cleared my throat and proceeded to spill my guts. I told them about the trip downtown, and the Gatsby party. I told them about counting out the money with Stew and Lewis and Nagle. I told them everything I could remember, except the part about getting snubbed by the two dolls.

"Isn't it standard operating procedure to turn in lost items at the end of a shift?" Duncan said.

"Yes," I said.

"Then why didn't you do that instead of going back to the theater?"

"Because I'm human."

I don't think they bought it.

"I figured the girl would need the money," I said. "She didn't even have a coat."

The cops glanced at each other.

"She didn't bring a coat with her?" Duncan said.

"No."

"Why not?"

I felt like Jon Voight being grilled by James Dickey. This happens to me a lot. I looked the cop in the eye and said, "I ... don't ... know."

Duncan started nodding. It was one of those minuscule-though-protracted nods that cops perform when they're thinking things over. He needed only a wad of chewing gum to complete the effect.

"You say she was drunk?" he stated.

"I would say that she was very drunk."

"Did anybody see you drop her off at the theater?"

"About eighty people."

He began nodding again.

I figured I had told them everything I knew about that night. It was time they told me everything they knew.

"Is the girl in trouble?" I said.

Duncan looked down at me. "We don't know. She's missing."

This made me feel bad. I wasn't kidding when I said I was human. I had seen too many cop shows to have any illusions about missing girls.

"You're the last person known to have seen her," Argyle said.

This made me feel bad in a different way.

"We're talking to anyone who knows her or has seen her in the past week," Duncan said.

"Am I suspected of doing something bad to her?" I said.

That wasn't quite how I intended to phrase it, but it caught the gist.

"Her parents reported her missing last night," Argyle said. "This is just a preliminary investigation."

I was impressed by the fact that he hadn't answered my question. Or had he?

"We want you to stay available if we need to ask you any more questions," Duncan said.

Which is to say: don't leave town.

"I'll be glad to help you any way I can," I said. "Glad" was stretching it a bit. "Willing" might have been the best word.

"Thank you for coming in and talking to us, Mr. Murphy," Duncan said.

He told me I could go. I got up and walked out of the office feeling embarrassed. I hate it when people call me "Mister Murphy." It makes me sound like a hand puppet.

When I entered the on-call room, Lewis and Nagle were standing in front of the cage. They saw me come in, and they gave me "the eye." Only it wasn't just "the eye," it was the worst "the eye" I had ever gotten from anybody.

"You can go up now," I heard Rollo say quietly.

Lewis and Nagle walked slowly past me, continuing to give me "the eye." I couldn't look them in the eye. I walked over to the Coke machine and started digging through my coat pocket for some change, but I couldn't find any. I gave it up. I walked over to the cage and looked at Rollo.

"Did Lewis and Nagle come in to get new tires?" I said.

Rollo shook his head no. "Hogan called them in off the road."

I started to say, "Yeah?" but didn't.

"Lewis was in line at the Sheraton Hotel down in the Tech Center," Rollo said, "and Nagle had been waiting in the taxi line at DIA for two hours."

I closed my eyes and nodded.

"Are the mechanics working on my tires?" I said, looking up.

"They haven't gotten to it yet," Rollo said. "There's a lot of people in line ahead of you."

I nodded again, then walked away from the cage. I entered the hallway and walked down to the doorway that led to the garage. I looked through the window on the door. Two taxis were up on racks getting their tires changed. The mechanics were rushing around. It looked like a NASCAR pit. Three more taxis were parked outside in the snow. I turned back and went into the on-call room. I thought about going out to 127 and getting my paperback book, but instead I just sat down at one of the tables and leaned back in the chair and stared at the wall.

The girl was missing, and I was the last person known to have seen her. I replayed the trip from the moment she had gotten into my taxi until the moment she had disappeared into the crowd. I hadn't seen her go into the theater. I hadn't seen her wave to anybody. She had just melded with the throng. I asked myself what the hell was the matter with me? If she had been a friend I would have made her go back into her apartment and get a coat. If she had been a friend I would have taken the pint of vodka away from her. She was just a kid. I had always liked to think of myself as "a friend of the teens." I like teenagers. I sometimes wish I still was one. Some people tell me I still am one.

Whenever a teenage fare asks me for advice, I keep it real, as the kids say. I tell them to listen to their parents. I tell them to stay in high school and get their diplomas. I tell them to do whatever it takes to get into college. I tell them that college is the last best deal they might ever get in their lives. I dragged my college career out to seven years, I liked it so much. And yet I had let that little girl get out of my cab with nothing but a bottle of vodka to keep her warm. I hadn't even checked to see if she had her purse, much less a coat. I could have given her one of my coats, either my "big" coat or my Rocky jacket. As I said, I keep my coats in the trunk since I never wear a coat in my cab. I put one on only when I open the trunk, depending on the weather and the amount of time I'm going to be outside of the cab. Forty-seven seconds on average.

And now the girl was missing.

I heard footsteps on the stairway. Lewis and Nagle came into the room. They didn't give me "the eye." They only glanced at me, then walked out the door. I didn't have time to read their eyes. Maybe I didn't know my eyes after all. Maybe I wasn't a friend of the teens. Maybe I was a fraud.

"Murph."

I looked up. Hogan was standing in the doorway. "I need to talk to you."

I got up and followed him into the hallway, trudged up the stairs and entered his office. He shut the door, then went around behind his desk. He didn't offer me a chair. For one moment things almost seemed normal.

Hogan removed his pop-bottle eyeglasses and rubbed at his lids, then he put them back on and looked up at me.

"I just spoke to our legal department on the phone," he said. He rubbed his lips with an open palm, then shook his head once. "Basically, you've been suspended from driving."

My mouth dropped open a fraction of an inch. This was similar to the times in my life when I had gotten fired, except then my mouth dropped a whole inch.

"If those cops think I know something about the missing girl, I don't. I told them everything, Mister Hogan."

He got a pained look on his face. This was the first time in fourteen years that I had called him "Mister Hogan."

"It's not that, Murph. I believe you. They do, too. But it's this purse thing. The legal department told me that you broke a serious rule when you didn't turn the purse in right away. You made a mistake when you drove back to the theater. You should have turned the purse in to the lost-and-found."

He leaned back in his chair and sighed.

"It's the insurance company. Legal told me that until this business with the girl is cleared up, you won't be allowed to drive. The insurance people won't cover your bond. Everybody's running scared."

I just stood there and stared at Hogan. I had tried not to think about it until then, but all bets were off. If the girl turned up dead, I was through with cab driving forever and I knew it. No taxi company would ever hire me again. No insurance company would okay it. This was the best job I had ever had in my life and it was hanging by a thread.

"Can I ask you something?" I said.

"Sure, Murph."

"Do you know who this girl was?" I meant to say "is" but it came out wrong.

"She's the daughter of a rich man," he said. "I can't tell you anything else."

I nodded. "Her parents reported her missing yesterday," I said. "That's why the cops are investigating a missing-person case after only one day, isn't it? Her parents are rich."

He nodded, then said, "Listen Murph. I feel bad about this. But I can't discuss the details with you. The detectives gave me a thumbs-down on that. I'm not allowed to tell you anything. You've been suspended until further notice. I'm sorry."

I looked around the room like I was looking for something. Then a thought entered my mind that was so evil that I'm ashamed to admit it, but it went like this: I could really use that twelve hundred dollars right now.

Like I said, I'm only human. You don't know the meaning of the word "human" until you've been "broke."

But it was just a passing thought. Money does that to humans. Clouds their minds. I've never had anything against the rich. I've spent twenty years trying to get rich writing novels. That's about as clouded as a mind can get. But all of a sudden a small patch of fog parted. I looked at Hogan.

"Do her parents know about me?" I said. "Do they know I was the last person to see her?"

Hogan didn't say a word, but his eyes were spilling their guts. "What does her father do for a living?" I said. "Run an insurance company?"

He shook his head no, then said, "I'm sorry Murph. I can't talk about these things. As soon as it gets cleared up, I'll personally call you at home and tell you to come back to work, even if I have to wake you up in the middle of the night."

"Try two in the afternoon," I said. "That's when the unemployed sleep."

I turned and walked out the door. I shouldn't have said that. Saying things like that is one of the many ways I have alienated practically every friend I ever had. I really could use an anger management course.

When I got back downstairs, I headed for the door. I intended to walk out and never come back. That was how I did things whenever I got fired from real jobs.

I stepped outside the on-call room and tried to slam the door shut, but it had one of those hydraulic pump things. The door sort of thumped closed. I stood there in the snow staring across the parking lot. After awhile I hung my head. I looked at the snow gathering on the toes of my Keds. Cab driving was the only hope I had left in life. There was nothing else I could do. I had tried everything, including a white-collar job. It almost killed me. Or maybe it was the chain smoking. I turned around and opened the door and went back inside.

I felt ashamed when I walked up to the cage. I wondered why I felt ashamed of trying to hang onto my only hope in life. There are better things to be ashamed of.

Rollo was watching me warily. If there had ever been a moment during the past fourteen years when a showdown between Rollo and myself was due, this was it.

But—"I got suspended," was all I said.

Neither Rollo nor his eyes said anything. I had a feeling he already knew though. Hogan would have informed him on the intercom: Rocky Mountain Taxicab #127 was in official lockdown from Murph.

"I guess I'll be back in a few days," I said. "Hogan told me it was just temporary. He said he would call me and let me know when I could come in." My voice was hoarse. It felt like toothpaste being squeezed out of a tube.

Rollo nodded. He didn't say anything. I felt like begging him to talk. Come on, Rollo, give it to me—a little malicious condescension. For old time's sake. I may never pass this way again.

But he just nodded and gave me a brief smile.

That almost did me in.

I turned and walked out the door.

CHAPTER 9

As I drove back through the snow, I started thinking about bread-lines. Unemployment does that to me. I started thinking about all the photographs I had seen that were taken during the Great Depression, all those men standing in long lines at soup kitchens, all those pictures taken by Margaret Bourke-White when she and Erskine Caldwell wandered around the South looking for poor people to take snapshots of, all those poverty-stricken folks who had been deliberately sought out and recorded for posterity.

But the more I thought about it, the more I began to wonder why photographers had to get in their cars and travel hundreds of miles just to find the Great Depression. I mean, if it wasn't right outside the window, did it really exist? I started thinking that I could get a camera and drive around and find some poor people to prove that another Great Depression had fallen upon us, or else I could go photograph some rich people to prove that the streets of America were paved with gold. I was probably in shock when I was thinking these things, but I couldn't stop thinking about them.

When I got back to my apartment building there must have been four inches of snow on the ground and it didn't look like it was going to let up. I realized I wasn't all that brokenhearted about not having to drive that day. After I got inside my crow's nest and put away my taxi gear and stuffed my loose cash into my *Finnegans Wake,* I cooked a hamburger and sipped a beer and started thinking about the Great Depression again. Unemployment rose to twenty-five percent during the Depression. This

I learned in a UCD history class. With luck I could probably name ten things that I had learned in grade school, high school, and college, and that was one of them. And I thought, *So what?* That's twenty-five percent of the workforce, not twenty-five percent of the American people. Statistically speaking, if you counted everybody in America—the housewives and children and old people—practically nobody has ever worked. But that still left seventy-five percent of the workforce working. It wasn't like everybody in America was lying in the gutter chewing on leaves. I began to suspect that the Great Depression was a hoax. This was what I thought about as I sat at the kitchen table chewing on my hamburger and sipping my beer and watching the snow get deeper on the rooftops of Denver.

I thought about what it would be like if I had worked at a factory during the Great Depression and the factory closed and I was told I couldn't work anymore, that I had to go home and sleep till noon and then sit on the front porch and do nothing until it was time to walk down to the breadline and get some free food. No wonder they called it the Great Depression. It sounded great to me.

I finished my burger and did the dish, then I went into the living room to check the TV schedule. I wasn't used to watching TV on a Wednesday, but I found that it wasn't much different than watching TV on a Tuesday. This was comforting. As I was channel surfing up in the high numbers where the public-access crowd hangs out, I nearly collided with the Employment Channel. I stopped to circle back around and take a look.

The Employment Channel is like the classified ads in the newspaper, except it's narrated by some guy with a job and takes longer to get through. Plus you can't mark the ads with a red pen. But I sat and watched for a while. It had been fourteen years since I had done this, and I wondered if the endless search for work had changed. I won't bore you with my conclusion. Then I wondered if people really did find jobs on the Employment Channel. I imagined thousands of people grabbing their telephones and dialing the number at the bottom of the screen as if it was a radio call-in contest: "Who sang *96 Tears*? We'll take caller number eight!"

After I got out of the army I received six months worth of unemployment compensation, which I felt was ironic because I had never thought of the army as a job. You can quit jobs. I got paid three hundred dollars a month to be in the army, and after I got out I was paid two hundred and seventy-two dollars a month unemployment to not be in the army. I knew a lot of sergeants who would have paid me twice that amount to not be in the army.

I continued to surf, and found to my dismay that not one channel was showing *Gilligan's Island*. I was lonesome for Mary Ann. I turned off the TV and stared at the wall for a while, then finally admitted to myself that I was at a place where all cab drivers dread being, even if they won't admit it. I was at that place where The Little Dream comes true. The Little Dream is an adjunct to The Big Dream, which is to get rich writing a novel. The Little Dream is to find some free time to write, and by the looks of things, I was going to be writing for a long time. I cursed the legal department of Rocky Cab, then got up and went to my steamer trunk and opened it up.

I keep my unsold screenplays on the right side of the trunk, and my unfinished novels on the left side. Then there's my unpublishable novels which act as ballast at the bottom. I never look at the unpublishable novels anymore. Some of them are both uncompleted as well as unpublishable, which is like the red-hot core of magma at the center of the earth. I never descend to that level anymore—I almost died of asphyxiation one night reading a bottom manuscript that I had written in college. It was during my John Barth period.

I don't know why I do this. Every time I leaf though my manuscripts I feel like I'm going to come across something that has promise, something that just needed time to ferment before it "took off." I don't even have to open the trunk. I know exactly where every manuscript is and what it's about. I feel like a man visiting a cemetery. Here lies Uncle Hemingway. He died during my sophomore year. Here's the crypt where Draculina rests in peace, a rejection slip driven through her ivory breast.

I once had a close encounter with Thomas Pynchon but managed to dodge that bullet by taking a college course that explained recombinant DNA, which theoretically could be used to create human mutations. You're probably way ahead of me by now—I'm talking lizard people! When I got home from the first class, I slid Pynchon back onto the shelf next to Donald Barthelme and got to work cooking up characters whose arms could grow back like lizard tails if they got yanked off by hay-baling machines. That took care of Chapter 1. I wrote about two hundred pages before I finally admitted to myself that I ought to incorporate a plot, but by that time the semester was over and my knowledge of farm implements had been depleted. It's a story as old as Gutenberg. The unfinished ms. (manuscript) went into the steamer trunk next to Draculina.

I closed the lid, went back to my chair, sat down, and started thinking about writing something new. But the problem with thinking about writing something new is that you're thinking about nothing because there's nothing there to think about. You have to think something up. It's like wandering around with a big magnet in a room full of wood.

Pretty soon I was thinking about the missing girl. I had been thinking about her all this time, I just wouldn't admit it to myself. I was thinking about all the things I might have done that would have prevented this situation. I was thinking that the reason all of this had happened was because of money. I had jumped a bell near quitting time because I wanted to pick up a few more bucks. I wasn't thinking about the girl at all, her well-being, her safety.

But then I thought that if it hadn't been me, it would have been some other Rocky driver who took her to The Flicker. That was the thing. It was the thing I had always been good at: weaseling out of blame.

But it didn't matter. It was out of my hands. It had been in my hands last Monday and I had blown it, and now it was out of my hands. All I could do now was hope that Duncan and Argyle found her alive and returned her to her parents. Then I could start driving again. I could start making money again. So it all came back to money. But what was money except a one-way ticket to food? And food was the means of survival. You ate food so you could hang around long enough to eat some more food. That was what I thought about: the complete dismantling of the entire structure of western philosophy—it's all about nothing but hanging around, Plato.

I got up from my chair and went for another beer. It wasn't even noon yet, and here I was drinking beer. I picked up the schedule for the film festival and looked it over, then glanced out the window. There must have been five inches of snow on the ground by then. I had considered going to see something avant-garde that afternoon, but I didn't want to drive in the snow. But then isn't this how it always is? A baseball game, a picnic, a wedding in the park—you plan it all, and then splat.

I could have called a taxi, but that just made me think of the missing girl, and of my job status, and food, and Plato. I hate losing my mind before noon.

Then the phone rang.

Normally I don't answer phones. But Hogan had promised to call if my suspension was up. I listened to it ring a few times, trying to find it not hard to believe that all my problems had been solved. But it was too hard, and I can't abide the ringing of a phone anyway. Prior to that day, whenever the phone rang I would simply pick up the receiver and set it back on the cradle, and it wouldn't ring again for a week. I don't know why anybody calls me. I never call anybody except the pizza joint.

"Hello?"

"Is this Mr. Murphy?"

It set my teeth on edge. I almost hung up. But maybe it was the RMTC legal department, or else the Colorado lottery.

"Yes."

"I hope I'm not disturbing you. My name is Randolph Hightower. I spoke with the managing supervisor of the Rocky Mountain Taxicab Company a little while ago, a man named Mr. Hogan. I asked how I might get in touch with you, but he told me you were not driving today."

I listened to this seemingly pointless recitation with little interest, except the part about Hogan, whose name was the only reason I didn't hang up. I had always gotten along well with Hogan. He spoke to me, on average, a little more than once a year, usually when it was time to get my annual physical. I would say that during the previous fourteen years we had spoken perhaps twenty times. He's the best supervisor I ever had.

"Yes," I said.

"Mr. Murphy, I hope you can spare me a few moments of your time. This about my daughter Alicia. According to a report I received from the Denver Police Department, you drove Alicia to The Flicker last Monday night. Mr. Hogan told me that two detectives from the Denver Police Department spoke with you earlier today about this."

I closed my eyes and slumped against the wall. This was exactly why I never answered my telephone.

It was as though all the telephones I had never answered in my lifetime had come together to form one giant, awful call. I came to within a hair's breadth of moving to Wichita. But this was the missing girl's father, and now I knew her name: Alicia Hightower. A rich man's daughter.

"Yes sir, I'm the taxi driver who drove your daughter to The Flicker last Monday," I said. I didn't want to use the girl's name. I felt I had no right to use her name. But beyond that, I was trying to keep this conversation on the highest plane of formality as possible. I didn't want to get any more involved in this business than I already was.

"Mr. Murphy, I wonder if it would be possible for you and I to meet?"

So much for that plan.

"Well I don't know," I said. "Mr. Hogan told me that the police advised him not to talk to me about this business. The police might not want you and I talking about it either."

"I'm not interested in what the police have to say about anything involving my daughter," Mr. Hightower said in a voice so cold-blooded that it reeked of money. I liked that.

"I told the police everything I could remember about last Monday night," I said. "If you have any questions, I could answer them for you right now. I would be more than willing to do that."

There was a moment of silence at the other end of the line. Then I heard him talking to someone else in the room. After another moment he said, "It's not so much myself but my wife who would like to talk with you, Mr. Murphy."

I wanted desperately to say, "Please, call me Murph," but I didn't.

"Mr. Hogan told me that you were not working today, so I was wondering if it would be convenient for you to come to my house," Mr. Hightower said. "I live on east Eighth Avenue, not far …" and he paused for a moment, "… from where you live."

He knew where I lived. But that did not come as a surprise. He knew my home phone number, my supervisor's name, and my employment status.

"I suppose we could meet some time," I said, trying to sound distant and disinterested, which I always do when talking to strangers outside my taxi. But this was the missing girl's father. I tried to tone down the "distant" while maintaining the "disinterested" because I really was disinterested, though not in a petty, cruel, or unkind way. I'm just never much interested in anything.

"The snow is pretty deep right now," I said. "I really don't want to drive my car in a blizzard."

"I could send my chauffeur over to pick you up," he said. "That would be no problem at all."

I almost started laughing. You might find this hard to believe, but I've never been very good at talking my way out of getting involved in terrible situations. I'm much better at getting sucked into terrible situations and then "winging it." This guy wasn't going to turn loose of me, but it didn't bother me the way it did when people attached themselves to me at parties, bars, or the ten-items-or-less line at grocery stores. And I knew the reason why: he was the father of the missing girl, the girl whom I had let down because all I ever cared about was money.

Mr. Hightower said he would send a car right over.

CHAPTER 10

I put on my "big" coat and closed up my crow's nest, but instead of going downstairs by the fire escape I took the interior stairwell, which I usually try to avoid because there's a risk of running into one of my neighbors. I don't know how many people live in my building and I don't want to know, but it must be about a dozen. The manager is a kid who goes to a free school to study things like macramé and yoga. His name is Keith. He's in his mid-twenties. He giggles a lot when he talks, but I don't think it has anything to do with drugs. He just seems naturally happy. Don't get me started on happy people. Myself, I only giggle when I talk when I'm drunk, but Sweeney usually puts a stop to that by threatening to call a cab, or my Maw. The last time he followed through on a threat to call my Maw was last St. Patrick's Day, but apparently Maw was at Duffy's Pub in downtown Wichita.

The stairwell inside my building is carpeted, so I managed to make the square spiral down to the ground floor without attracting the attention of the residents making muted thumps and moans beyond the wooden doors.

I stepped out into the frosty winter afternoon. The snow seemed to be abating, but by then there were six inches on the ground. The TV weatherman would probably report three inches. I've never seen a weatherman yet who knew what a window was.

I didn't have to wait long for my ride. The streets were silent, there was no traffic, but then I heard the musical jangle of chains, and I figured this must be the rich man's chauffeur. When you've driven a taxi as long as I have, you get to know your chain music. These were coming fast, and pretty soon a monstrous black four-wheel drive vehicle came around the corner making mincemeat out of Mother Nature's contribution to the legend of the Mile-High City. I noticed that there were ski racks on the roof. Don't get me started on skiing.

The Jeepster pulled up at the curb, the big tires blasting the snow out of the gutter like a speedboat making waves. I liked that. I was in the presence of money. George C. Scott said it best in *Patton*: "Man has conquered the ocean and the mountains," but Patton was really talking about money. The Big Money. Tax dollars, if you want to get technical.

The chauffeur hopped out, and he looked exactly like one. Shiny black boots, black riding breeches, black jacket and gloves, and a black saucer cap as handsome as anything worn by a Yellow Cab driver. I do like those Yellow caps. I was wearing a knit job on my own head. Now that I was suspended, I didn't feel right wearing my Rocky cap. And I wouldn't have felt right wearing it into the home of a man whose daughter a Rocky driver had let down.

"Mr. Murphy?" he said, as he came around the front of the vehicle. He was young and good-looking. We had something in common. We both drove for a living.

"Please," I said, as I trudged through the snow toward him, "call me Murph," please.

"All right, Murph, if you want to hop right in, we'll get on the road," and the happy chap held the rear door open for me.

I've held cab doors open for plenty of people, both men and women, but I had never thought about how it made the men feel. It made me feel kind of helpless and stupid. But I guess the rich are used to it.

I climbed into a wad of warmth, a plush backseat with carpet on the floor. The chauffeur hurried around to the driver's side and climbed in. "It shouldn't take more than ten minutes to get to the Hightower residence," he said, as he adjusted his mirror and began fiddling with buttons on the dashboard. "Mr. Hightower told me to offer you a drink if you would care to have one," and a little door flipped open in front of me revealing a small bar. It was built against the back of the front seat—and I'm not talking two-ounce shooters, I'm talking the "big" bottles.

"Thanks, but I'm fine," I said. I couldn't remember the last time I had turned down a drink, but then I couldn't remember the last time someone offered me one.

"How about a little music?" he said, as he put the locomotive into gear and pulled away from the curb. He switched on what seemed to be a quadraphonic stereo system "... *myyy ba-bee does the hanky-panky ...*" but I asked him to turn it off.

"What's your name?" I said.

"Jeffrey."

"Mind if I call you Jeffrey?"

"Not at all."

We headed out across the white wilderness of Capitol Hill in the direction of 8th Avenue, toward a district that lies way, way east of where I live.

I'll admit it. Plush intimidates me. I couldn't bring myself to go into my "passenger" act and ask Jeffrey inane questions about what it was like to be a chauffeur for a rich man. So I just asked regular inane questions. "How about this Colorado weather?" I said.

"It's really something," he replied.

That was a fairly inane answer, so I figured we would get along okay.

I didn't know where we were going to end up. I imagined a place like the Richthofen mansion. An uncle of Baron von Richthofen, the German World War I flying ace, once owned an estate in east Denver. But the place we ended up was a residential mansion on 8th Avenue, tucked in between a lot of other mansions, the kind of houses that make me think of the word "upkeep."

A gate opened automatically. We pulled into the driveway, and one of three garage doors opened automatically. I caught a glimpse of a Rolls. You can carve that on my tombstone.

Jeffrey hopped out and opened my door and told me that Mr. High-tower was waiting for me in the library. He led me through a doorway into the mansion.

I'm not going to describe the interior of the mansion to you. You've seen them in plenty of movies. Use that imagination you're forced to use when your cable goes out and you have to listen to the Broncos on the goddamn radio. I'll describe the library though. There was a big fireplace with a fire going, and all the furniture appeared to be upholstered in pale green velvet, with mahogany arms and legs. I had delivered furniture in my youth. I know my arms and legs. This was a high-priced place to store books, and the walls were hidden behind plenty of them.

Mr. Hightower was seated in a chair in front of the fireplace. He was wearing a white sweater, one of those loose jobs that golfers wear. I didn't notice the rest of his getup. Golf clothing clouds my mind. He was holding what looked like a fresh drink in his right hand, except the ice was almost melted, as if he hadn't gotten around to taking his first sip. He was staring at the fire.

"Mr. Murphy is here, Mr. Hightower," Jeffrey said.

Mr. Hightower looked over at us, and the expression on his face was so hopeful that he might have been expecting his daughter to be with us. This made me feel bad. He set his drink on a small table beside his chair and got up.

"Your guest prefers to be called 'Murph,'" Jeffrey said, just before he quietly eased out of the room and shut the door. We were getting along just fine.

"Thank you for coming ... Murph," Mr. Hightower said.

"You're welcome, sir," I said, as he shook my hand.

"Let me take your coat," he said, then pointed at a small couch near the fireplace. "And please, have a seat."

I removed my coat and hat, and he took them to a closet while I sat down. I was about as uneasy as I had ever been in my life, and that's going some. It reminded me of my first confession at Blessed Virgin Catholic Church in Wichita when I was seven—and all the confessions that followed.

"Would you like something to drink?" he said, when he returned.

"No thank you, sir, I'm fine," I said. I wanted to keep what wits I had left. I could feel them scrambling for the exits.

He turned his chair around to face the couch, then he sat down.

"I want to thank you so much for coming, Murph," he said. "I spoke on the phone with Detective Duncan a few minutes ago, and he told me there hasn't been much progress in finding my daughter. They're still interviewing people. But I want to tell you right off that this isn't the first time my daughter has disappeared without telling anyone where she was going. I'm worried, you understand, but it was my wife who called the police as soon as Alicia's roommate Melanie told us that Alicia hadn't come home from the movie on Monday night."

He paused and looked down at the floor, then shook his head and looked up at me. "My wife is distraught. She asked me to invite you over here since you were the last person we know of who spoke with Alicia. She seems to think that you might provide some clue as to her whereabouts."

As Mr. Hightower spoke, I felt myself going through the sorts of changes that I go through whenever a fare climbs into my cab. As I had told Alicia, being a cab driver is a lot like being an actor. Every time a fare gets in, I quickly size him or her up using the mental Univac that all cab drivers possess, and decide how I should act in order to optimize my tips. I don't know that this is so very different from what normal human beings do in social situations, but until I became a cab driver I didn't really care how I acted around strangers, which would explain why they never tipped me.

My Univac was humming in overdrive as Mr. Hightower described the situation, and pretty soon it spat out a card that said, "act mature."

It was directing me into a realm where the air was thin. As far as I could recall I had never been there before, and I feared the journey would be cold and lonely.

A door opened on the far side of the room. A woman walked in, and right away I could tell that she had been drinking. I didn't need my Univac to tell me this. I'm third-generation Irish-Catholic.

She crossed the room with the posture and bearing of someone who is making a conscious effort to hide her drunkenness, a kind of subtle stiff-bodied grace, like a nervous actor going onstage in a serious drama.

I found myself rising from my chair. Apparently my Univac had taken over the social amenities.

Mr. Hightower rose and went over to her, took her hand, and escorted her to a loveseat where she sat down.

"Thank you, dear," she said turning loose of his arm and clasping her hands on her lap. She held her torso erect.

"This is Beverly, my wife," Mr. Hightower said. "Beverly, this is Murph. He's the cab driver who chauffeured Alicia to the theater last Monday night."

"How do you do, Murph," she said, in a voice both soft and strained, enunciating each word.

I nodded. "Please to meet you, ma'am," I said. I found myself sitting back down on my chair.

"I was just telling Murph that I spoke on the phone to Detective Duncan a few minutes ago," Mr. Hightower said. He didn't sit next to his wife. He sat down in the chair by the fireplace. I had to turn my head to look from one to the other as they spoke. "He had nothing new to report."

Mrs. Hightower nodded to her husband, then turned her gaze on me. "Was Alicia alone when you picked her up?" she said.

"Yes, ma'am," I said, surprised to hear her ask this. I glanced at Mr. Hightower, who was giving me what I can only describe as a "noncommittal" stare. I found myself speaking before I fully thought through an idea that was forming in my mind. It was intuitive, you might say. "I was under the impression the police had already told you everything that I had told them," I said.

"Well, yes ..." Mr. Hightower said. "It was difficult ..." he glanced quickly at his wife, "... to garner any real sense of what went on that night by listening to a police report. My wife and I would like to hear it from you personally, if you wouldn't mind retelling your story for us."

"I don't mind at all," I said, and I didn't mind. But I detected a sense of strain in Hightower's every word. He seemed to be on edge, which was understandable, but there seemed to be something else behind it that I couldn't make out.

So I told them. Having already rehearsed with Duncan and Argyle, I was not only able to tell it better, but to add things that I had inadvertently left out. During the first go-round I had simply described the action, but now I was getting down to the details like a good unpublished novelist.

"She was alone when she came out the door," I began, and spent the next five minutes describing the cab ride. Then I spent ten minutes describing my fruitless efforts to track Alicia down at The Flicker and the Gatsby party. When I mentioned the Gatsby party, Hightower looked at his wife and said, "Worthington." Mrs. Hightower nodded. I noticed that a handkerchief had appeared in her right hand and she was dabbing at her face.

Hightower glanced at me and then said, "The party was thrown by J. Lawrence Worthington, a business associate of mine. He's on the board of directors of the Mile-Hi International Film Festival."

I nodded, which is something I had learned to do when people told me either uninteresting or incomprehensible things. I continued with my narrative, which ended when Stew tucked the purse into a paper sack and stapled it closed.

"This morning I was called into Mr. Hogan's office where I was interviewed by Detectives Duncan and Argyle," I said. "They told me that they were searching for Alicia, although they didn't tell me her name."

By now Mrs. Hightower was weeping discreetly, and was having trouble holding her torso erect. I had never in my entire life wanted so badly to be somewhere else, and that included high school.

Mrs. Hightower dabbed at her nose and said, "She did not mention at all whom she might be meeting?"

"No ma'am. She just said she was meeting some friends."

I noticed that Mr. Hightower had finished off his drink. I hadn't noticed it when I was reciting my narrative, but then writers, even unpublished writers, have a tendency not to notice what's going on around them when they are the center of attention.

Mr. Hightower was holding the glass in an odd way, with the tips of his fingers of both hands pressed against the glass. He was staring down into the drink, but every so often he would glance at his wife and then look away. As I say, he seemed troubled by something other than the obvious.

Mrs. Hightower took a deep breath and gave out a sigh that caused her shoulders to sag. Mr. Hightower quickly got up and crossed to the loveseat. He sat down next to her and put an arm gingerly around her shoulders. "You see, dear?" he said. "Murph here has told us everything that the police told us."

She began nodding with her lips tucked between her teeth. She looked at me and said, "I thought perhaps some minor detail that the detectives had overlooked would give us a clue as to her whereabouts."

I began nodding my head in unison with hers. Mr. Hightower sat rock-still. I ran his body language through my Univac, but even that reliable machine couldn't determine whether his stance was disapproval or something else, so I stopped nodding and started talking. "I know what you mean, ma'am. As a cab driver I hear a lot of stories second hand,

and second-hand stories can be like a bad Xerox. Or ... or ... maybe a translation of a novel from French to English might be a better way to put it. You know, I mean, you get the translator's version rather than the original artist's." I suddenly felt that my tendency to rely on analogies was as superfluous as ever. I decided to get back to the point before I started talking about rock climbing. Not that I had a rock-climbing analogy handy, but I bet I could have thought one up fast. "Anyway, if you have any questions, I'd be happy to expand further on anything that took place that night," I said, hoping she wouldn't take me up on the offer.

Mr. Hightower turned his head and looked right at his wife. She was looking down at the handkerchief in her lap. She was plucking at it. "Alicia forgot her purse, but she remembered to take the bottle of vodka with her," Mrs. Hightower said softly.

"Yes ma'am," I said quietly.

She began nodding again, nodding in the way that Detective Duncan had nodded, the way all detectives nod when they're thinking things over. She took another deep breath and exhaled saying, "Thank you for coming here, Murph." Then she looked at her husband and said, "I think we should pay Murph something for his time, dear."

I sat rock still. I became embarrassed for her. I became embarrassed for her husband. Reducing every act of kindness to money is my job.

But Mr. Hightower simply squeezed her shoulder and said, "I'll take care of everything, honey. Why don't you go lay down? I'll be in to see you in a little while."

Mr. Hightower had finessed what could have been an awkward situation, and he had done it so deftly that I realized he was good at it. People who are good at things are people who have done the same things many times over.

I stood up as Mr. Hightower helped his wife to her feet. I watched as she picked her way across the room with that deliberate step of the secretly inebriated. I felt badly for everyone in this entire poor rich family.

Mr. Hightower returned to his chair and sat down. He looked at me silently for a few moments, then said, "Thank you for talking to my wife."

"You're welcome, sir."

"As I told you earlier, it was my wife who called the police. She did so without my knowledge. She was frantic. This has happened before. My daughter Alicia is very headstrong, and she has this idea that she is going to become an actress." He paused a moment, then looked me right in the eye. "I know where my daughter is."

CHAPTER 11

"If "I had known my wife intended to call the police I would have stopped her," Mr. Hightower said. "A year ago we were in France for the film festival at Cannes, and Alicia disappeared for two days. She was with a group of ..." he raised his right hand and flapped it like a flag, "... filmmakers that she had met. She was hanging out with them, making the scene. We managed to track her down. She hadn't really run away. Alicia is somewhat of an irresponsible girl. She doesn't always ... weigh the consequences of her actions, and I suppose it's because of the way she was brought up. I'm a wealthy man and she has always been a very protected girl. I think all young people possess a sense of immortality, but when you add the protective barrier of wealth to that illusion, you get a girl like my daughter. I'm wealthy and I know absolutely nothing about teenage girls." He glanced at the doorway through which his wife had just exited, then he looked at me.

"I didn't want the police involved in this at all, but when Alicia's roommate called to tell us Alicia hadn't come home from the movie, my wife immediately called the police." He looked at me somewhat apologetically. "That's how you got involved in this. But I do appreciate your coming over here to speak with my wife. She insisted I call you."

I sat there absorbing this monologue, then finally said, "Where is your daughter?"

He took a deep breath and sighed, then shook his head and said, "She's with a filmmaker. I know the man. Kid really. He's in his mid-twenties. He fancies himself a director. When J. Lawrence Worthington was drumming up corporate sponsorship for the Mile-Hi International Film Festival, I met this young director at a dinner party. My corporation made a large contribution. Worthington asked me if I would like to sit on the board of directors of the festival, but I turned him down. I'm on the board of directors of a number of corporations. I support the arts but I have no time to get deeply involved in that sort of thing. But Alicia seems to think that, because I am connected in a small way with the festival, she herself is a part of …" he flapped his hand again, "… show-biz."

"How do you know she's with this man?" I said.

"Because while my wife was getting the police involved, I had a private detective check out the director. Alicia is staying at his … 'film ranch,' I suppose he would call it. She became enamored of him at that damn dinner. She couldn't stop talking about the fact that he was a local filmmaker. He was the first person I thought of when I learned that Alicia had not come home from the festival on Monday night. She talks constantly about becoming an actress. The director had a movie in this year's festival. It's called *The Man Who Crawled Across Denver.*"

I froze.

Mr. Hightower looked at me and shook his head. "I own controlling interest in four corporations in Colorado, but I have never been able to control my own daughter … or my wife. I didn't want them to know that I was keeping such close tabs on Alicia, so when my wife called the police without consulting me, I couldn't very well tell them that I knew where she was. What a mess."

As he spoke, I no longer felt like I was sitting in the home of a rich man who was in complete control of his universe. I felt like I was sitting in the driver's seat of 127 listening to a fare on the way to DIA, a forlorn businessman whose latest deal had fallen through. I get a lot of those executives. I get all kinds of people in my taxi. It's like Grand Central Station. Every type, breed, species, and ilk of human being has passed through my backseat. I didn't need my Univac to tell me how to act now. I listened sympathetically, right up to the moment Mr. Hightower looked me in the eye and said, "I want to ask a favor of you, Murph."

My wits began searching for the exits. My steering wheel disappeared and I found myself trapped in the home of a rich man. I heard a faint ringing in my ears. It sounded like a faraway telephone. This happens whenever somebody asks me a favor—a phone begins ringing somewhere in my universe and I can't find it to lift the receiver and set it back on its cradle.

"Name it," I said.

He sat forward in his chair with his elbows on his knees and his hands clasped. "My daughter is eighteen years old," he began. "I can't tell her what to do. I want her to go to college but she's got her sights fixed on becoming an actress. I don't want her staying with this … filmmaker. She won't listen to me or her mother, but I would like her to go back to her apartment and stay with Melanie. And I was wondering if you would be willing to take her purse out to the film ranch. And tell her that we want her to leave that place and go back … home."

My mouth dropped open an inch. At least six replies occurred to me but none of them made their way out of my mouth before he said, "You could drive your taxi out there and return the purse. Just tell her that you found it in the backseat of your cab. I'll pay you for your services, of course. And if she asks you how you knew where to find her, tell her that I told you. She probably won't be surprised. And then … you could mention that we want her to … come back home."

My Univac plugged itself in and began going to work. "I'd like to do that," I said, "but there's one problem."

"What's that?"

"I've been suspended from driving my cab."

His mouth dropped open a bit and his eyebrows went up. "Why were you suspended?" he said.

"Because I failed to follow standard operating procedure and turn Alicia's purse in to the lost-and-found as soon as I got off work. Mr. Hogan told me that the legal department at Rocky Cab and the insurance company insisted that I be suspended until this case was resolved."

I saw anger break across his face, the kind of anger you see only on the faces of people who do not tolerate nonsense. I'm talking the worst kind of anger of all: rich anger.

"This is ridiculous," he muttered more to himself than to me.

Then it occurred to me that some of that anger might have been directed at his wife.

He sat back in his chair and looked at me. "Well, that's the end of that," he said.

I wasn't sure what he meant. But he clarified things.

"I'm going to call the police and tell them that we know where our daughter is, that we tracked her down. As far as your suspension goes, I'll make a few phone calls." His gaze rose above my head. He got a distant look in his eyes. I knew that look. He was thinking. I was in the presence of a man who had controlling interest in four corporations and God knew what else. You don't rise to that level of existence without thinking.

He looked back down at me. "Why don't we end this conversation right here, Murph. I'll get back to you as soon as possible." He pointed at a window covered by thick drapery. "With the snow as deep as it is, you wouldn't be able to do anything today anyway."

"Excuse me, sir," I said, "but do you actually have your daughter's purse?"

"I'll get it," he said, like a man who gets things. I nodded.

He nodded too, then ran the palm of his hand across his mouth, and in doing so wiped away the manifest anger. He smiled. "Nasty weather out there, Murph," he said. "Are you sure you wouldn't like a shot of something for the road?"

I returned the smile. "Jeffrey offered me a drink on the ride over," I said. "Maybe I'll take him up on it on the ride back. Your four-wheel drive has a nice stereo system, by the way."

"Alicia insisted we install it," he said. "She and her friends liked to listen to it whenever Jeffrey drove them to the mountains for skiing at our resort."

And then he said, "Do you ski?"

My Univac screamed at me to stay mature. I did my best.

"No, sir, I've never skied. I'm from Kansas."

"It's a wonderful sport," he said. "My father served with the Tenth Mountain Division ski troops during World War Two, and after he came back home he and some partners built one of the first ski resorts in Colorado. Sourdough Park. That's one of the corporations I'm involved with. If you ever want to try skiing, Murph," he said, knocking on the wooden table with a knuckle, "just let me know."

"You'll be the first person I call," I said, and I wasn't lying. Not exactly.

We stood up then. He shook my hand and thanked me for coming over, and for agreeing to help him with Alicia. He said he would call me the next day. I said a few agreeable things that I can't remember because a phone was ringing inside my head and someone was reminding me that I had taken a vow to never get involved in the personal lives of my fares. I think it was me.

As Jeffrey drove me back to my crow's nest, I managed to down three shots of whiskey. Jeffrey asked if I would like to hear some music during the trip, and I said sure. Brother, you haven't lived until you've cruised across the vast white wasteland of Capitol Hill sipping Glenlivet while Tom Jones belts out "… *I'll never fall in love again* … " on quad speakers.

I entered my building by the front door. Before I got halfway up the stairwell I heard my telephone ringing. I deliberately stifled the urge to race up the stairway, an urge instilled in all human beings by Alexander Graham Bell, that prick.

It was still ringing as I entered, removed my coat, dawdled over to the phone, and lifted the receiver.

"Hello."

"Murph. Hogan here. Good news. Your suspension has been lifted. You can come back to work."

"When did this happen?" I said.

"I just got a call from legal. They okayed it."

"Did the police find the girl?"

Hogan paused a moment. "I don't know. They didn't tell me anything about that. They just told me to take you off suspension."

"That's strange," I said disingenuously. "Why would they do that?"

"I really don't know. Maybe they did find the girl. It's probably best not to ask. Those lawyers live in a different world from us, Murph."

I nodded, then I remembered to speak. Phones are like math—use it or lose it. "Well, thanks for calling," I said.

"We put brand-new snow tires on one twenty-seven," he said. "They really hold the ice."

"That's good to hear," I said.

"So you're coming back to us, right?"

Until that moment I hadn't realized that Hogan might have been concerned that I had walked away from Rocky Cab for good. My parting shot had been aimed right at his heart.

"Sure," I said. "Either tomorrow or Friday."

"That's great," he said. There was another pause, then he said, "I'm sorry about all this, Murph. Most of us didn't think you did anything to that girl, except maybe Rollo."

Jaysus.

"Don't worry," I said. "It's Chinatown, Jake."

"Thanks, Murph."

We rang off.

I went into the kitchen and looked into my fridge and decided on a Coke. Up until I got the phone call from Mr. Hightower I had been planning on taking a mid-winter spring break. I'm talking beer and

Mary Ann. But the Glenlivet was as far as I was willing to go now. Tomorrow I might find myself doing a job for a rich man, and I wanted as many wits as I could corral. Wits and beer don't mix. Chocolate and beer do, but we've had that conversation.

I took my Coke into the living room and sat down in my easy chair, but instead of turning on the TV, I picked up the schedule for the Mile-Hi Film Festival. I wanted to take another look at the blurb for *The Man Who Crawled Across Denver.*

It was produced, directed, and written by someone named Antoine Baroni.

I hadn't paid any attention to the credits when I saw the movie. As much as I love film, I never pay any attention to the credits. If you want to see a real dog-and-pony show, go to the theater at the Denver Center for the Performing Arts sometime and watch the audience at the end of a movie. The way they sit rooted to their seats while the credits roll, you would think the second coming of Christ was on the bill. I'm the only person I've ever known to get up after the fadeout and walk to an exit. The film buffs throw me angry glares from the corners of their eyes—as if I care who the executive producer was on *Zabriskie Point.*

The blurb didn't tell me anything about Antoine Baroni though, and neither had Mr. Hightower. There were a lot of things he hadn't told me about this situation, like where the film ranch was located. I had never heard of any film ranches in Colorado. I knew there were a few production companies around town because I had driven their employees in my cab. Every once in awhile a production company comes out from Hollywood to do a movie in Denver, and the town goes nuts. But most of Denver usually ends up on the cutting-room floor. I know three Yellow Cab drivers who had bit parts in movies that needed taxicabs in certain scenes. Hollywood never asks Rocky Cab to provide bit players. They always go to Yellow Cab, the bastards.

I tossed the program aside and stared at the gray/green face of my TV, wondering who Antoine Baroni was. After awhile I got up and went to my phone book, dusted off the cover, and looked up his name. There were a lot of people named Baron, but no Baroni. I figured it for a pseudonym. I didn't blame him. He wouldn't be getting any offers from Hollywood based on his screenplay. Me and Antoine Baroni had something in common.

CHAPTER 12

It was Friday. It was noon. The streets of Denver were dry. The sun was out. It might as well have been June. The four brand-new snow tires were humming on the melting asphalt. I was headed east along Colfax Avenue in Rocky Mountain Taxicab #127, trying to figure out Colorado weather. Lying on the shotgun seat beside me was a white purse containing twelve hundred dollars and a tube of lipstick. I was looking for a dream factory. A small one located somewhere in Aurora. I had been given the address by Randolph Hightower, whose eighteen-year-old daughter Alicia was staying with an independent filmmaker named Antoine Baroni. My mission? Return the purse, and maybe—just maybe—return the daughter to her roommate.

I had visited the Hightower mansion on Thursday evening when the thaw had commenced and the gutters of Denver had been filled to overflowing like a spring runoff. Cars were stranded in flooded underpasses. People were standing on the roofs of their vehicles waiting for firefighters in rubber boats to rescue them. I saw it all on TV. It was better than *Gilligan's Island*. I only hoped the firefighters had sense enough to explain internal combustion to the geniuses standing on their roofs.

I drove farther east. I left Denver's city limits and entered Aurora, the enchanted suburb. A lot of liquor stores, a lot of used-car lots, a lot of pawnshops, a lot of everything that keeps the wheels of free enterprise greased. I passed the Aurora Fox Theater. It's one of my favorite movie theaters. It's a big Quonset hut. It was built after World War I. It reminds me of mops. I would hate to mop the Aurora Fox. That's where I saw *Jaws* first-run. I don't want to talk about it.

I kept going. I passed Fitzsimons Hospital. That's where Dwight Eisenhower recuperated from his heart attack in the 1950s. I try not to think about Dwight Eisenhower. I kept going. Pretty soon I was out of the city, if you think of Aurora as a city. I sometimes do. I entered the countryside. Fields. Horses. Cows. The works. I was looking for an address of what had once been a farm. I hate looking for those kinds of addresses. I'm a city driver. Farms aren't like cities. The addresses are painted on boards nailed to fences. Okay. I'll concede it. A lot of city addresses are painted on boards nailed to fences, but farm fences are different from city fences. I never see roosters sitting on fences in downtown Denver. I once saw a monkey sitting on a fence in downtown Denver but I kept driving.

I had learned more about Randolph Hightower on Thursday night when I went over to the mansion to get the purse that I was to deliver to his daughter. More than I wanted to know, in fact. I learned that he owned a golf course. He asked me if I ever played golf. I said no. That ended that conversation. He also told me he had attended the Colorado School of Mines in Golden, where he had received a degree in engineering. He owns a corporation called Hightower Engineering. It's involved in the oil-shale business. My mind went slightly blank when he began describing the oil-shale business. I felt like I was sitting in Algebra class back in high school. I nodded a lot as he spoke. The nuns had taught me how to nod. I nodded my way through four years of high school.

I finally found the address. It was painted on a mailbox. The mailbox was at the entrance of a dirt drive that led toward a big house a quarter-mile into the property. The property was fenced off but it wasn't much of a fence, just a simple two-rail job to remind the cows where the edge of their world ended. I guess it doesn't take much to intimidate a cow. I wouldn't know. I avoid anything that weighs more than a Volkswagen and has teeth.

But I didn't see any animals. This didn't appear to be a working farm. According to Hightower, Antoine Baroni referred to his place as a "film ranch." He had inherited the place from his parents, who were dead. Hightower knew Antoine Baroni, had met him at the fundraiser for the Mile-Hi International Film Festival. Baroni had aspirations of becoming a big time movie director. He would have been better off raising cows. His epic short-subject *The Man Who Crawled Across Denver* enjoyed only one showing at the Ogden.

I had checked the festival program again on Thursday because I had been thinking about going to see it one more time. I wanted to see the movie from the perspective of someone about to meet the director. I didn't know what I expected to see differently in the film, but it didn't matter. Antoine Baroni's flick had been featured once, and that was it. I checked the newspapers for reviews but there was no mention of it, no critique, no insights into the mind of a man who had made such a movie. But I knew one thing: I liked the movie. What that said about me remained to be seen.

I drove along the dirt drive that led toward the big house. There were a lot of shade trees surrounding the house. I didn't get a good look at the place until I was right in front of it. I had been expecting the kind of house that might have been homesteaded by the Fabulous Furry Freak Brothers, but it was a well-built place, though old. Two stories. Shingled roof. It looked like a home once owned by a man who had raised cattle for money, and was not just a flophouse for hippies. Thirty yards farther down the road was a smaller house. The white paint was flaking away on both structures. There was a sense of ruin about the setup, but not total ruin. It was obvious to me that the word "upkeep" had packed its spurs and skedaddled years ago.

I parked and shut off the engine. I looked in my rear-view mirror. It was time to put on my game face. I was just a cab driver returning a piece of lost luggage, a clueless man in a baffling landscape looking for a former fare.

I grabbed the purse and climbed out of my cab and strolled up to the screened porch bearing a look of both confidence and innocence, neither of which I possessed. For all I knew, a band of crazed hippies might be watching from the windows, prepared to panhandle. But in my T-shirt pocket I had a small plastic nasal-spray bottle containing ammonia. That's just between you and me. Rocky Cab doesn't allow drivers to carry guns. I'm pretty sure the city of Denver doesn't either, but I know for certain that Rocky Cab doesn't. Ergo, the ammonia.

I climbed the steps to the screened porch, entered the porch proper, and went up to the front door of the house and gave it a few quick raps like a harried cabbie eager to get shut of a small errand. I lifted the purse and looked down at it like a cabbie slightly baffled by the fact that he was even holding a purse. As I say, being a cab driver is a lot like being an actor. This may explain the affinity I felt for taxi driving when I first started out. I've spent my whole life pretending not to be me, and generally succeeding.

Someone was moving around inside the house. I reached up and touched the ammonia bottle. I've never drawn the weapon in the line of duty, although I have made a few embarrassing mistakes with it that I'm not going to describe.

The door opened an inch and I saw a single eye peering at me.

"Yes?"

"Hi there," I said, my voice cranked high-pitched and fast, "I'm a Rocky Cab driver and this purse was left in my taxi the other night and I've been trying to locate the owner to give it back to her." I hoisted the purse so the eye could see it. "I guess the girl's name is Alicia Hightower and I was told she might be here and I was just wondering if you happened to know where she is."

The eye got big. It was no longer looking at me. It was looking at the purse.

"Seems there's a hell of a lot of money in the purse and my boss told me to get it back to her as quick as possible, so if you could let me know where she is I'd sure appreciate it."

The door opened a little farther. I saw two eyes and part of a face full of hair. Hippie hair from where I stood. Wet hippie hair. A single naked arm snaked toward me and the wet man said, "I'll give it to her."

I eased the purse out of his reach and said, "I'd like to let you do that but my boss told me specifically to give it to Alicia Hightower, so if she's here I'd sure appreciate it if you could have her come to the door so I could give it to her." I was doing a kind of Gomer Pyle, light on the Mayberry.

"She's not here," he said. I dropped the Gomer.

"Where is she?"

The eyes frowned. The arm went back inside the house. The guy glanced back inside and said, "Could you give me a minute? I'll be right back."

I didn't want to say yes. I wanted to say no. This was the Yin and Yang of the moment. Did I mention the fact that his arm was covered with droplets of water? I was sure the sonofabitch was naked. I shrugged. "Okay, but I got to run out to my cab and call the dispatcher to let him know I found the house, so I'll be out in my cab when you get back."

I wasn't doing Gomer now, I was doing Murph. I left the screened porch and went down the steps and climbed into my cab and shut the door and locked it and started the engine and waited for Antoine Baroni to come out shooting.

Maybe it hadn't been such a good idea to mention the money. But then maybe it had. I just didn't have enough experience with crazed wet hippie directors to know what to do in this situation. I was "winging it."

After two minutes he stepped out onto the screened porch wearing a red flannel shirt and blue jeans and sandals. He was wearing glasses, too. His hair looked like it had been given a quick rub with a towel. So did his beard. I knew the look. The UCD theater department offered classes in various aspects of film production as well as film theory and criticism, and I had taken a few of the classes back in the days when I was busy cashing free checks. Antoine Baroni looked like every student filmmaker I had ever seen at UCD. He came down the steps and walked up to my cab. I cracked the window. I didn't bother to explain why the engine was running. I never explain things to people who don't give me money.

"Sorry," he said. "You caught me in the tub."

"Where's Miss Hightower?" I said.

Antoine had an anxious look on his face. "She's asleep right now."

"Maybe you should go wake her up."

"I'd hate to do that," he said.

"All right, but I'll have to call the dispatcher and tell him that I wasn't able to return the purse and that the management at Rocky Cab will have to turn the purse over to the police and let them take care of it for us. Thanks anyway."

I was winging it all right. I was soaring.

Antoine shoved his hands into his pockets. It was cold out here in the wild east even if it looked like summer. He squinted at me through his glasses. Then his eyes zeroed in on the purse lying on the shotgun seat.

"I guess I could wake her up," he said.

"That's a good idea," I said.

He turned his head and looked down the road toward the small house. "Or maybe she's awake by now."

I looked down the road at the little house. "Is that where she's sleeping?"

"Yeah."

"Okay, well, why don't I just run my cab down there and see if she's up."

Antoine cleared his throat, then looked anxiously at the little house. My sense that he was a crazed hippie was fading. I wasn't getting any "bad vibes" from him, as the hippies used to say. But he did seem nervous.

"Listen," he said. "No reason to bother her right now ... is there any way you could leave the purse with me? She told me that she lost the purse, but I guess she didn't know she left it in your cab. I guess she didn't remember."

I paused a moment before I answered. "Why wouldn't she remember that?" I said.

He cleared his throat again. "Well, she'd been drinking when she lost the purse."

An honest answer. I liked that. It bent my twig in a new direction. "Is your name Antoine Baroni?" I said.

He looked surprised and said, "No."

"It's not!" I exclaimed. I really did. I exclaimed it.

"No, that's just a name I use in my … my business," he said. "My name is Toby Brown."

"Is your business movie making?" I said.

He grinned and looked down at his sandals, then nodded. I felt like I was making progress, though in what direction I wasn't sure.

"Did you make a movie called *The Man Who Crawled Across Denver?*"

His face seemed to collapse. By this I mean it was like someone had removed the poles from a tent, leaving the canvas sagging. I know a thing or two about that. Did I ever mention that I was in the Boy Scouts? I know all about sagging tents.

But his was an expression of stunned surprise.

"Yes I did. How did you know?"

"I saw your movie at the film festival on Tuesday."

He nodded slowly, then said, "But how did you know I made the film?"

I was hoping I wouldn't get around to that. During the past minute I had been getting the feeling that Antoine Baroni wasn't the brightest spotlight in the studio, but maybe I was wrong. "Alicia's father told me," I said.

Antoine stood fully erect and nodded. "Oh. Her father. Is that how you knew my name and how to find her?"

I nodded. I didn't want to say anything more. Not right then. I pretended I was talking to a cop. Or a lawyer.

Antoine looked toward the little house, then looked around at the drive that led to the big house. His hands were still in his pockets. He looked down at me. "Are you working for that private detective?" he said.

"What private detective?"

"The private detective who was out here on Wednesday pretending to be a furnace inspector?"

"I work for the Rocky Mountain Taxicab Company," I said. I reached up to my visor and yanked my Herdic license away from its metal clip. A Denver taxi license is called a "Herdic" license. Don't ask me why. "Here's my license," I said.

He didn't look at it. He just nodded and said, "Alicia told me that every time she runs away from home, a furnace inspector shows up pretending not to be a private dick."

I shrugged. "Her father told me where to find her," I said. "She left her purse in my cab last Monday night. I'm just trying to give it to her. I'm no dick."

He nodded in the direction of the little house and said, "Come on. She's down there."

I put the Herdic back on its clip, then said, "Do you want to climb in shotgun?"

"Nah, I'll walk."

He began trudging down the road in the direction of the house. He looked sort of downcast and forlorn. I kept the shift in low and idled along behind him. Pretty soon I pulled up in front of what I would later learn was his studio, the headquarters of his production company, the throbbing heart of his mighty film empire, and the cutting room where he had edited *The Man Who Crawled Across Denver.*

CHAPTER 13

I parked 127 and watched as Toby went up to the door of the house, which up close looked like a quaint cottage, although there was no wisteria in sight. He tried the doorknob but it didn't work, so he ambled around to one side of the cottage and peered through a window. He came back around to the front and said, "She's asleep on the couch."

He reached into a pocket and pulled out some keys and went to the front door, inserted a key and eased the door open.

I grabbed the purse and climbed out of 127 and walked up to the door. Toby was inside now. I looked in. There was a lot of film equipment scattered around the room, tripods, lighting kits, your standard dream-factory tools. Toby was standing by an old couch looking down at a body wrapped in a blanket. The hair looked familiar to me. Flapper hair. I watched as he tapped her shoulder. It took a few taps. She awoke with a gasp and looked up at him. I saw fear in her eyes. This didn't surprise me. Whenever I wake up, my fear lasts until I finish shaving.

"They found your purse, Alice," Toby said.

Alicia, or Alice, blinked a few times, then sat up with the blanket still wrapped around her like the leaves of a cheap red cigar embroidered with yellow ponies. "Who did?"

"The cab company," and he pointed at me with a thumb.

Alicia looked toward the doorway where I was standing with the purse held in plain sight. She didn't look at me. She looked at the purse. Then she threw the blanket off. She was wearing a red flannel shirt, blue jeans, and tennis shoes. They looked like they fit Antoine better than they fit her. I didn't see the flapper dress anywhere. It had been four days since I had last seen it. She stood up fast and ran toward me with one hand outstretched, reaching for the purse. I yanked it away from her grasp.

"Are you Alicia Hightower?" I said.

She looked startled, not at my question but at my refusal to let her take the purse.

She dropped her arm and looked up at me with, like, total exasperation. I'd seen that look on a lot of women's faces. Alicia didn't look like a woman though. She looked like a little kid in baggy clothes. She parted her mouth, cocked her head at an angle, and glared at me with, like, totally wide eyes. Yes, I do know that look. Some people call it "disgust."

But then her expression changed. She recognized me. I recognized her recognition. Her eyes got less wide, and her mouth closed.

I continued with my fake interrogation. "The woman who left this purse in my taxi last Monday was dressed like a flapper," I said. "You don't look like her."

Her eyes zeroed in on the purse again, then she looked up at me. "I'm Alicia Hightower," she said. "That's my purse."

"Do you have any identification?" I said. Her face went blank.

"This purse contains some money," I said. "If I turn it over to the wrong person, I might get in trouble with my boss."

Alicia turned her head, glanced at Toby, then looked back at me. "Toby knows who I am."

I nodded. "What's the address of your apartment back in Denver?" I said.

She parted her lips to speak, then clamped them shut. "I'm not going to tell you my address."

"Well, I'm going to need some I.D.," I said. "I can't just give you this purse. I might get in trouble."

I looked at Toby. He was standing there watching this routine with his hands shoved deep inside his pockets. He still looked forlorn.

I raised my eyebrows.

"Tell him where you live, Alice," he said.

She told me her address.

"Okay," I said, and I handed her the purse. She snatched it out of my grasp. She opened it wide and looked inside, then yanked the wad out. She flipped through it with one thumb like she was used to examining wads of money, then she turned and hurried back to Toby. "It's all here! You can make the movie!"

Antoine glanced quickly at me and did a kind of "squeezy" thing with his teeth and cheeks. He raised his palms as if to quiet Alice.

I didn't need a film festival program to tell me where that money was headed. But it was none of my business. While Alicia was hopping up and down on her toes and fanning the money in Toby's face, I cleared my throat and said, "I brought something else for you, Alicia."

She turned fast and looked at me, her eyes wide with anticipation. I rarely see that on a woman's face. "Your father said he wants you to come home."

Her tent collapsed. She unfanned the money, stuffed it back into the purse, and snapped it shut. "Thank you for returning my purse," she said in a voice as fine and polite as anything ever produced by a finishing school, yet containing a dreary undertone that might be aimed at a boorish lout. But the girl didn't know what she was really dealing with—an asphalt warrior.

"I think your father just meant he wanted you to go back to your apartment and stay with Melanie," I said.

The condescension evaporated and she looked slightly ashamed. I liked that.

"I'm eighteen years old," she said. "I can do anything I want."

I glanced at Toby. He looked uncomfortable. I couldn't tell whether I liked that or not. The fact that Alicia had been sleeping in the cottage rather than in his house spoke in his favor.

"I'm just passing on a message to you, that's all," I said. "Your parents had the police looking for you."

"They called the police?" she said, her eyes going wide again. So did Toby's.

"Yes they did," I said.

"Why did they do that?" she said.

"I don't know," I said. "Maybe they love you."

She lowered her eyes and began fiddling with the clasp on the purse. Toby finally decided to step onstage. He looked at me and raised his right hand, a small gesture of conciliation, and said, "Listen, I ... we appreciate your returning the purse. I'll be glad to pay you whatever it cost for you to drive out here."

I shook my head no. "Mr. Hightower took care of that. I've got my money and you've got your money. I guess that takes care of that. I'm finished with my delivery."

I turned and walked out to my cab.

As I was opening the door I heard the door to the cottage slam shut. I looked back. Toby was coming toward me, his hands in his pockets.

"Thanks again for bringing the purse back," he said.

"No problem," I said.

He looked down the road. The anxiousness had returned to his face. "Do the police know she's out here?"

I thought this over, then decided to tell him as much as I thought he needed to know. "I don't think so. Mr. Hightower told me he was going to call the police and let them know he had tracked down his daughter. He's known she was here ever since ... well ... since that furnace inspector dropped by."

Toby nodded. I wondered for a moment why he was worried about the police, but the answer came to me quickly; he was normal. Who wants the police nosing around? The guy was a filmmaker, though. Maybe he had drugs. I didn't want to know. I never want to know anything.

"She came here Monday night," Toby suddenly said. "I couldn't get her to leave."

"Why not? What's keeping her here?"

"She was afraid to go home. She lost the twelve hundred dollars and she didn't want her dad to find out."

Alicia may have been eighteen years old but she had the mind of a seventeen-year-old.

"Did you and Alicia go see *The Great Gatsby* that night?" I said.

"Yeah. We were supposed to go to a costume party afterward, but we didn't get there. She wanted to discuss a movie I've been wanting to make."

"Can I ask you something else?"

"Yes."

"When the movie was over, did you leave by the front door or the side exit?"

"The side exit." I nodded. Let's move on.

"Is Alicia going to be in your movie?" I said.

He said yes, then looked down the road—the road to Denver.

I now knew that the money was a part of this deal. And she came with her territory. "Can she act?" I said.

He shrugged. "She told me she had a part in a high school play."

"*Carousel,*" I said.

"That's right," he said. "Did her dad tell you that?"

"No. She told me on the night I drove her to The Flicker."

Toby sighed. He reminded me of the kid in the raccoon coat. The world was filled with men and women.

"So she's going to stay here, huh?" I said.

"I guess."

"How long?" I said.

"I don't know."

"I'm only asking because her father will want to know."

He nodded.

"Do want a lift back to your house?" I said.

"Okay." He went around and climbed in shotgun. As I drove him back to his house I looked over at him. "I liked your movie," I said.

He smiled. "Thanks."

"What are you going to do with it?"

"What do you mean?"

"Will it be distributed?"

"No, it won't be distributed. That was just a one shot deal. I know a filmmaker who runs things for the festival. He worked it into the program for me."

It was a short trip. I pulled up in front of his house, and my hand automatically went to the flag to shut off the meter. You can't take the cab out of the cabbie. I didn't know if he had noticed me do that, but I felt stupid, so to cover my gaffe I said, "I've been trying to write screenplays for fifteen years."

He looked over at me, and suddenly I wished I hadn't said that. I was willing to bet he ran into guys like me all the time. I've read plenty of stories and seen plenty of movies about it—anyone associated with the movie business finds himself cornered sooner or later by a novice writing screenplays in his spare time. I felt like a rube.

"But then all taxi drivers write screenplays," I said. "It's one of the two requirements for driving a cab. The other is having a clean motor-vehicle record. Before Rocky Cab certified me to drive, I had to prove I knew how to format a screenplay. I failed the test twice."

He smiled.

"But I haven't sold anything," I said. "Thank God that's not a requirement."

"Well, good luck," he said. "It's a tough business."

I was glad he said that. He had smoothed over my gaffe. Few people had ever done that for me. By "few" I mean "none."

He opened his door part way, then looked down the long road to Denver and said, "Oh Christ," and shut the door.

I looked down the road. A car was coming. "What's the matter?" I said.

Toby raised his hands, removed his glasses, and began rubbing his eyes. He put them back on and lowered his hands and watched as the car got closer. "It's my crew," he said. "They worked on *The Man Who Crawled Across Denver.*"

The car pulled up directly in front of 127, blocking my way. This annoyed me. But I didn't have time to express my annoyance before the crew came piling out of the car like a thousand clowns. They headed for both sides of my cab, four young men and a young woman.

"Oh no ya don't!" one of them yelled on Toby's side.

"Where do you think you're going?" someone yelled on my side.

"What the hell is this?" I said.

Toby looked at me. "They haven't been paid yet."

Oh yes. Money. Artists one and all.

I put 127 into reverse and let the engine idle us backward ten feet. The clowns stayed with us. Then one of them made the mistake of pounding on my hood.

I shifted 127 into park, shut off the engine, and opened the door. When I stood up from the cab I was holding the microphone in my hand. "Send a police car!" I shouted into the mike. "I'm being attacked!"

The artists went silent. I liked that.

I reached up with my left hand and withdrew the nasal spray just in case. I wasn't too worried, but I did know that withholding money from an artist was as dangerous as toying with a nun.

They had stopped their pounding and shouting but they were trembling with rage. Their eyes were glued to the mike. I lowered it to my heart and said, "The police are on their way."

Then I heard the shotgun door open. Toby got out and closed the door. The crew swarmed around him.

"You're not going anywhere until you pay us, Toby!" the tremblingest of the crew said. His face was red.

"Yeah, Toby, where do you think you're going!"

They each performed a variation on this theme, including the female of the chorus, who sang the loudest. In my limited experience, angry women artists are the most volatile geniuses to deal with. "You owe us nine hundred dollars!" she shrieked.

"Which one of you hit my hood?" I inquired. "The insurance company will want to know your name."

They froze.

It's an interesting thing about money. It possesses its own laws of physics, one of which resembles the Doppler Effect, or the "red shift" as it is known in astronomical circles. For instance, when money is coming toward you, it makes you feel good. When it's moving away from you, it makes you feel bad. The fact that I was able to freeze this crowd without actually saying the word "money" indicates how awesome the gravitational pull of money truly is. It's like a black hole, only green.

"I don't know what the problem is here but somebody is going to have to pay for that dent," I said, pointing at the hood, which, of course, had no dent.

"I did not do that," one of them said.

"I didn't either," another said, backing away.

Their bond of rage was being dispersed like atoms in a cyclotron. I love science. Pretty soon a tall fellow was left standing alone in front of Toby, looking both defiant and guilty, as well as familiar. I recognized him. He was the man who crawled across Denver.

Then I heard someone shouting. I turned and saw Alicia running down the road toward us. She was waving something in an upraised hand. Something the color of green.

CHAPTER 14

Alicia arrived at the scene of my bluff breathing hard and shaking the twelve hundred dollars in her fist. "I've got your money right here!" she said.

Toby did that subtle hand signal of silence again, but it didn't shut her up. He started to look truly forlorn. She stuffed the wad into his hand. "Go ahead and pay these people," she snarled. "Then tell them to go away."

The electrons moved back toward Toby. These control subjects would have been ideal participants in a physics project I had failed in high school.

"You owe us nine hundred dollars, Toby," the girl said again.

I mentally tried to divide nine hundred by five but fumbled on the four. I failed a lot of things in high school.

Toby seemed to know what he was doing though. He began peeling off one-hundred-dollar bills and dispersing them like neutrons. I may not be any shakes at math but I have a pretty good eye for long green. I noticed that he handed three bills to the crawling man—the star of the show. I had mixed feelings about that. As a film fan I felt he deserved the money, but as a cabbie whose hood had been used as a bongo drum I felt like messing with his mind.

"Who's going to pay for my hood?" I said.

Alicia glanced at me with inquiring eyes, then looked at my hood. Everybody looked at my hood.

I set the mike on the seat and walked around to the front of 127 and began rubbing at a random spot with my fingertips. "I'm going to be in plenty of trouble if my boss sees this."

The crawling man came forward and leaned down and looked at it. "I don't think I did any damage," he said, his voice fraught with uncertainty.

"The insurance company might disagree with you," I said.

He was rattled. He was clutching those three bills like a drowning man clutching another drowning man.

Then a short guy with a trim beard approached and said, "I really don't see any reason to get the police involved in this. Maybe the appropriate thing to do would be for each of us to pay for a part of it." He looked scared. Everybody looked scared. Everybody except Toby.

This short guy with the beard though, I knew his type: reasonable. Every once in awhile I encounter reasonable people in my line of work and I always feel sorry for them. They're fighting a losing battle.

I decided it was time to bring down the curtain on this melodrama. The fact that I sympathized, and even empathized, with their artistic plight—being shafted out of a paycheck—was countered by the fact that I had never liked bullying of any sort, especially when an individual acquires his courage by becoming part of a faceless mob. I always say, if you need false courage, get it out of a bottle like I do.

"I guess there isn't much damage," I said. "The boss probably won't even notice it."

I walked around to the driver's seat and picked up the mike. "Cancel that police call," I said. And then for effect I said, "Ten-four," and tossed the mike onto the seat.

I looked at the crawler and said, "You know, you shouldn't go around touching other people's stuff."

He nodded and looked down at his money, then mumbled, "You're right, I'm sorry."

"You're lucky this guy was here," I said, pointing at Mister Reasonable, who began nodding and smiling and finally saying, "Well, we got what we came for so I think it would be best for all of us to leave right now."

They left in a hurry. Piled into their car and went away.

I watched their dust.

Toby came up to me and said, "I know a lot about sound equipment. I've used radio-controlled mikes in my movies. But I've never seen a taxi radio work without turning on the transmitter first."

I raised my chin and smiled at him. "I've never seen a film crew work without pay, but then I'm not a movie producer."

He nodded and looked down at the three remaining hundred-dollar bills in his hand. Three little raisins in the sun.

"I guess I'll get going," I said. "Good luck with your next film project. I look forward to seeing it."

I didn't look at Alicia. I got back into 127, started the engine, and pulled away. As I cruised down the long road to Denver, I glanced in my rear-view mirror and saw Toby and Alice watching my trail of dust. I sighed. "Show-biz," I said aloud, then set a course for a mansion on east 8th Avenue. I had one last stop to make. "After all this is over, I am never again going to get involved in the personal lives of my fares."

He said.

I parked in front of the Hightower mansion and got out. There was an intercom on the gate. I had used it on Thursday. I pressed the button, and after a few moments I heard the voice of Mrs. Hightower say, "Yes?" I told her it was me. She believed me. The gate swung open. It made me feel important. I glanced back as I entered the grounds, hoping somebody would notice me. I had done that on Thursday, too. I don't know what made me think the rich neighbors would be impressed by a taxi driver passing through a gate. Maybe it was my ego.

When I got up to the door it was already open. Mrs. Hightower was waiting for me, and I immediately sensed that she had not been drinking.

There's something about sober people that makes them seem normal. I've always found it interesting that there are varying degrees of drunkenness but only one degree of sobriety. I've never met anyone who was too sober. Nuns maybe. I took off my Rocky cap and entered the foyer.

"Did Alicia say that she would leave the ranch?" Mrs. Hightower said as she closed the door.

A knife in my heart right from the get-go.

"No, ma'am. I returned her purse but ... and I told her what your husband said but ... and she seemed all right but ... I guess she's going to stay."

I saw a bit of life go out of Mrs. Hightower's eyes. "Why don't you come into the library and tell me what happened out there," she said. She led me down the hallway, and all the way there I was doing the fastest edit in the history of movies. There was a lot I wanted to leave on the cutting-room floor, especially the scene with the crazed crew. I hoped that Mr. Hightower would be present, but the library was vacant when we entered. "Is Mr. Hightower home?" I casually inquired.

She turned and smiled at me. "My husband was called downtown on some business. He asked me to apologize if you arrived before he got back. He may not return until late."

She pointed at the chair by the fireplace. "Would you care to have a seat?"

I crossed the room and sat down with my cap in my hand.

"Would you like something to drink?" she said.

"No thanks, ma'am, I'm fine."

I waited for her to offer herself one, but she crossed the room and sat down on the loveseat and clasped her hands on her lap. "How is Alicia?"

"She was just fine, ma'am. In fact she was sleeping when I got there." Then I wished I hadn't said that. It didn't sound right. I thought it would sound healthy. Sleep is good. My edit was falling apart. I quickly told her about the cottage down the road from the house. "Have you ever met Toby Brown?" I said.

She frowned slightly. "I believe I met him at the Mile-Hi Film Festival dinner, but I don't quite recall."

I leapt past that remark and told her that Toby Brown seemed like a nice guy. "Antoine Baroni is just his directorial pseudonym," I said.

"Why would anyone need a pseudonym?" Mrs. Hightower said. "Is he better than the films he makes?"

I couldn't tell if this was sarcasm or an innocent query made by someone who knew nothing about the egos of artists. I decided to file it in my mental Rolodex under S for sarcasm. I might use it some day.

"I've seen only one of his films and I liked it," I said. "He seemed about the same as his movie."

"Did you tell Alicia that we wanted her to go back to her apartment and stay with Melanie?"

"Oh yes, ma'am, I made that quite clear." I was starting to talk like her. I couldn't help it. I'm a cab driver. "I received the impression that she and Toby are planning to make a movie together."

"With Alicia's twelve hundred dollars I suppose," she said, and I knew right then that Mrs. Hightower was no fool. She was married to a rich man. She understood money.

"I think so, ma'am."

"Does my daughter really believe that a movie can be financed with twelve hundred dollars?"

"I don't know anything about movie making, ma'am," I lied. I knew a few things—like for instance a movie couldn't be financed with three hundred dollars. I wished Mr. Hightower was there.

"I performed in a movie once," Mrs. Hightower said.

I froze.

"I aspired to become an actress when I was a girl," she said. "When I was in high school I won the female lead in a production of the musical *Carousel*."

When she said that I felt like I had the lead role in *Vertigo*. But I managed to smile and nod. Mrs. Hightower got a sort of vacant look in her eyes, the look of someone remembering something that she had lost a long time ago, and I don't mean her car keys.

"I attended the same prep school as Alicia," she said. "The Colorado School for Young Ladies. Every year since nineteen fifty-six they have staged *Carousel*. When Alicia was a senior she won the lead role, too. I was so proud of her. But it went to her head just as it went to mine."

Her eyes came down out of the past and she looked directly at me. "I went to Hollywood and managed to get a role in a grade-B movie called *Summer Kicks*. My screen name was Beverly Burke. I quickly learned how difficult it is to shape an acting career. I came back to Denver soon after that and married Randolph. That was the sum and substance of my aspirations to be an actress. And now Alicia is following in my same foolish footsteps." She glanced at the liquor cabinet, then looked at me. "We want her to go to college, but she has no interest in schooling. She's a grown woman now, and unfortunately has the legal right to make up her own mind."

She glanced at the liquor cabinet again, then looked down at her hands. I sensed that this meeting was over and that she wanted me to leave. I'm pretty good at sensing when people don't want me around. I didn't learn it as a cab driver though. I was ten years old when people started avoiding me.

"If there's anything else I can do for you, ma'am, please let me know," I said. "I guess I had better take off. I still have a few hours left on my taxi shift."

"Of course," she said. She arose from the loveseat. "Thank you for all you've done, Murph. I'll tell Randolph what you told me."

I stood up. "You're welcome, ma'am." I started to say that I hoped everything would turn out fine, but that's not how I talk. I never have the slightest hope that anything will ever turn out fine.

"I'll show you to the door," she said.

"You don't have to do that, ma'am. I know the way."

"All right, Murph. Thank you for everything. It was very pleasant getting to know you. Goodbye."

I was surprised that she didn't walk me to the door. It's the rare woman who will let me wander around inside her house alone. But I wasn't surprised when I heard the distant clink of a bottle as I opened the front door. I stepped outside.

I wasn't lying when I said I had a few hours left on my taxi shift, although I would have lied if that's what it would have taken to get out of there. It was almost two in the afternoon when I pulled away from the Hightower mansion, and I had been on duty for seven hours. On Thursday evening I had told Mr. Hightower the details of my getting suspended, and how I had made only seven bucks before my near-accident. The upshot of the deal was that he offered me two hundred dollars to do this favor for him, one hundred to make up for the fact that his wife had played a role in getting me suspended, and another hundred to drive out to the film ranch.

I like saying the word "upshot." I wonder where it comes from.

Mr. Hightower had told me that if I felt uneasy about doing the job that he would understand, and if so, he would send the private eye out to return the purse. But I told him I had served two years in the army and wasn't afraid of artists. That may have been pure bluster, but I wanted a two-bill payday. Sometimes I'll do practically anything for lots of money.

I had leased 127 that morning and grossed seventy-five dollars in hotel fares before going out to the film ranch, so I was doing all right for a Friday. So all right that I became filled with lethargy. I could have driven another five hours, but I decided to call it quits for the weekend. The next day was Saturday. I had two days off before I had to think about earning money again. Nothing makes me lazier than having money. I would be a terrible millionaire.

I've read about guys who win a million bucks in the lottery and a year later they're broke and can't figure out what happened. But to tell you the truth, I couldn't see myself spending a lot of dough even if I did win the lottery. A cabin on a mountaintop with a 52-inch color television is my idea of the American Dream. I'll probably never achieve it but what the hell—if I could hook a coaxial cable into my brain right now and watch 500 TV shows simultaneously, I would drive only on weekends.

CHAPTER 15

Saturday was the last day of the Mile-Hi International Film Festival. The weather was cold but clear. I was planning to go to the Esquire Theater at two in the afternoon and catch *Vertigo,* then make it over to The Flicker where they were showing *Psycho.* And then, depending on how willing I was to face angry glances, I would walk over to the DCPA theater to catch *Shadow of a Doubt.* I planned to drive my Chevy this time since I didn't trust any of the cab companies including my own to get me to The Flicker on time. Of course, this meant that I would be going to the movies sober, something I generally try to avoid doing because it diminishes my ability to ignore the director's personal vision.

I'm still up in the air about the validity of the auteur theory. On the one hand there is no doubt that Hitchcock was the puppet master on all his greatest films, but on the other hand I doubt if he turned on the water during the infamous shower scene. So what does it really mean when the critics say "auteur"? It probably means I should ignore the critics. But then who am I to question the intelligence of people who don't make movies?

With the exceptions of the animation festival and the short-subject program, I had missed most of the contemporary films being introduced or heralded at the festival, but this did not really bother me. It had been a long time since I had been impressed by what the critics call a "must-see" film. I hate to think of myself as a cinematic curmudgeon, but it seems to me that "must-see" is just a label the studios slap onto all their releases nowadays, sort of like the Surgeon General's Warning. Who takes it seriously? My idea of a "must-see" film is something like *Dr. Strangelove*, which came out when I was a kid. My Maw wouldn't let me go see it. Somehow she had known that Stanley Kubrick had directed "that jiggle movie" *Lolita*, and she wasn't about to give me fifty cents to see a Kubrick film with the words "love" and "strange" in the title. So I didn't get to see it until I was in college. Imagine my disappointment when I discovered that it wasn't a jiggle movie.

After *Vertigo* ended, I sped over to The Flicker and got in line for *Psycho*. The cashier who had given me grief on the previous Monday was behind the counter again. When I stepped up to buy a ticket, I looked her right in the eye. I knew she would recognize me. She didn't. It made me feel unimportant.

After *Psycho* ended, I hung around in the lobby until I overheard a group of people talking about walking over to DCPA to catch *Shadow*, so I sort of tagged along behind them. I'll admit it. I didn't want to walk in the dark by myself after seeing *Psycho*. I had made that mistake once in college. I don't want to talk about it.

I rarely go to the DCPA theater. It's too hardcore. I don't mean porno, I mean they take their rules a little too seriously. When I was a student at UCD, I went to see *Scorpio Rising* with some buddies, and I wasn't aware of the DCPA smoking rules. I walked into the lobby with a butt dangling from my lips. A female usher was on me like a puma. "There's no smoking in here!" she barked. Maybe pit bull is a better analogy. I stepped over to a drinking fountain and doused the ash, then started to toss the wet butt into a trash can, but she charged my ankles again and barked, "You'll have to throw it away outside!" I had to go back out the front door and drop it into a trash barrel. I imagine life is like that in California nowadays.

When *Shadow* ended I looked around at all the film buffs silently staring at the credits. They looked like statues in the *Valley of the Kings*. I stood up and put on my coat and said, "Man, that was a good one!"

Then I made my way past the knees of the kings in my row saying, "I'm for some beer!" I saw a female usher charging down the aisle toward me so I escaped out a side exit.

I'm sorry, but I just can't take credits seriously. I would make a terrible film critic.

I walked back to my car in the dark, and only remembered to be scared of Mrs. Bates as I was inserting the key in the lock, but by then it was too late. I got in, started the engine, and sped off.

I had spent six hours watching classic movies, three of the finest suspense films ever made, the cream of the crop, so by the time I pulled into the parking lot of my apartment building I was thoroughly depressed. As I trudged up the fire escape to my crow's nest I couldn't help but think of all those screenplays lying in my streamer trunk. I had written quite a few unsold suspense films. Of course I've also written unsold action adventures, as well as unsold comedies. I don't want to get too redundant here, so I'll drop the word "unsold." I have never wondered who invented that word. I did.

I was so demoralized when I entered the darkness of my kitchen that I again forgot that Tony Perkins' mother was waiting for me with a butcher knife. I switched on the lights and opened the refrigerator and grabbed a beer on the way to the closet to hang up my coat. I put my coat away and sat down.

I thought about turning on the TV, but my eyes kept drifting to the steamer trunk. I used to tell myself that I should just throw away all my unpublishable manuscripts. When I was just starting out as a failed writer I used to save all my rejection slips. This was a game I played, in the way that little kids like to play "grownup." I have played all the games that writers play. I hung onto the rejection slips because they seemed to possess some sort of significance that began to elude me as I grew older. I suspect that most beginning writers keep their rejection slips for the same reason that wounded soldiers keep spent bullets that are pried out of their bodies.

You would be hard-pressed to find a literary game that I have not played. Writers are a lot like people who go to the dog track. They have countless theories and systems of betting, but it all comes down to the same thing: when the dogs cross the finish line, somebody else gets published.

That's why I started thinking seriously about writing a new screenplay that night.

Then the phone rang, thank God.

I "grabbed" it for the first time in years. It didn't even make it to the second ring.

"Hello?"

"Is this Murph?"

"Yes."

"This is Randolph Hightower."

My right arm almost went into the automatic hang-up mode, but I fought it like Peter Sellers. "Yes sir, what can I do for you?"

"I'm sorry to call you so late, Murph, but I've been trying to get hold of you all evening."

"That's no problem, Mr. Hightower. I was at the film festival catching a few movies."

"I see. I take it that you don't have an answering machine."

"No sir, I don't. I've never had one."

"This is off the subject and I hope you don't mind my suggesting this, Murph, but you might want to invest in an answering machine. I know it makes my life more manageable."

"Well, I'll certainly think about that, sir," I said, my vocal chords going into the automatic-response mode. I was barely aware of what he said after the word "invest." I rarely listen to people who use the words "Murph" and "invest" in the same sentence.

"The reason I'm calling, Murph, is to ask if you could tell me what went on when you visited the film ranch yesterday. My wife told me that you visited our house afterwards, but … she had a little trouble remembering a few of the things you told her."

I ran his tone of voice through my Univac and it spat out a card that told me what I already knew. So rather than try to recall the few things I had told Mrs. Hightower, partly because of my hack editing job, I simply described the visit en toto. By "en toto" I mean "todo el mundo." And that included the dog-and-pony show involving the mutinous crew.

"After the crew drove off, Toby had three hundred dollars left over, and I'm certain he had been counting on the entire twelve hundred to finance his next film project."

I heard Mr. Hightower softly whisper, "For the love of Christ."

I liked that.

"But I have to say, Mr. Hightower, overall, Toby did not strike me as a … a stupid person. To be honest, I got the impression that he would have preferred that Alicia return to her apartment. But at the same time I could tell that he wanted … or maybe needed … that money to do a film."

"I can tell you his financial situation, Murph." His voice was bitter. "He's virtually broke."

"I sort of gathered that by the looks of his property."

"This is just between you and me, Murph, but Tobias Brown stands to inherit a lot of money when he reaches the age of thirty. I had some people look into his background. That's where I was yesterday while you were visiting our house. They told me that his father's will stipulates that he be given a small allowance until he reaches the age of thirty. His father's bankers take care of the property and taxes. But Tobias is only twenty-six years old. He has four years to go before he can begin wasting his father's hard-earned money on movie making. His father was a very successful rancher."

I was a little shocked by these personal revelations. I had always assumed that rich people were fairly discreet when it came to discussing money matters, especially money belonging to other people. But what did I know about the rich? What did I know about life where the air is thin? The only thing I did know was that Randolph Hightower was bitter and broken hearted because his little girl was old enough to make her own decisions.

I recalled Alicia singing those lines from *Carousel* as I drove her to The Flicker. She didn't have a bad voice, but she didn't have a voice comparable to that of Shirley Jones. Shirley Jones was twenty-two years old when she starred in the movie version. I know a lot about Shirley Jones. I fell in love with her when I saw *The Music Man* at the age of twelve. She later played the mother in *The Partridge Family,* but I didn't realize it was her until after the show had been canceled. Her hair was different. Like I said, I never pay attention to the credits.

"Anyway," Mr. Hightower said with a sigh. "I want to thank you again for going out there for me, Murph. I'm indebted to you. If I can ever do anything for you, please don't hesitate to give me a call."

"Well ... if any of your employees ever need to take a taxi to DIA, I work Mondays, Wednesdays, and Fridays," I said with a small-though-practiced chuckle, trying to bring some levity to this rather sad dialogue.

"You can count on that," he said abruptly, all business now. Business was something he understood. "We generally call Yellow Cab for airport trips, but I will see to it that Rocky Cab gets all of our corporate calls in the future."

Yikes!

I was stealing fares from Yellow drivers and I wasn't even lurking at the mall.

"I appreciate that, sir. Thank you very much."

We said our goodbyes and hung up.

That was the end of that week.

CHAPTER 16

I slept badly on Saturday night, and it had almost nothing to do with Mrs. Bates. Every time I woke up I started thinking about Alicia Hightower in her flapper get-up and the fact that I had let her climb out of my taxi drunk and coatless. I thought about the interrogation by Duncan and Argyle, and how I had been worried that Alicia might turn up dead somewhere. My greatest fear in life is to be tried as an adult.

But mostly I was bothered by the idea that I had done a bad job of taking care of a fare. One of the reasons the Pubic Utilities Commission regulates taxis is for the safety of the passengers. Drivers are not licensed unless they pass a few tests, including a driver-safety program, the idea being that not just anybody can be allowed to chauffeur people around town without some kind of guarantee that the customers will arrive at their destinations safely. Admittedly it is a government guarantee, and I have never put much faith in government guarantees—I've always said, don't put the government in charge of it, whatever it is. But I could see that the PUC's well-intentioned intrusion into the free market had some arguments in its favor. In spite of their efforts to protect the public safety though, it still came down to the willingness of us independent operators to play the game by the rules, and maybe more importantly, by the spirit of the rules.

By this I mean that one of the easiest ways to get around blame is to obey rules to the letter, as well I know. But I also know that if something bad had happened to Alicia, I would have clung to that excuse for as long as it took to break me down and force me to come crawling back to myself begging my forgiveness.

I lay awake in the darkness thinking that I really wasn't much of an asphalt warrior. I couldn't shake the feeling that even though the Hightower business had come to a benevolent conclusion, it still wasn't over. On the Monday night that I had delivered Alicia into the hands of Antoine Baroni with no concern whatsoever for her welfare, I had simply been trying to pick up some quick bucks before turning my cab in for the night. I had let her climb out of my backseat and onto the mean streets of Denver without a coat, and clutching a pint bottle of vodka.

As far as I was concerned, this business was not over.

I felt as if the meter on 127 was still ticking, waiting for me to do whatever it took to raise my flag again. I heard that soft, almost plaintive, almost wistful voice of Alicia singing the song from *Carousel*, and I thought about the fact that her mother had won the lead role when she, too, was a girl.

When Mrs. Hightower mentioned that she had starred in *Carousel*, I wondered if Alicia had been lying to me. I wondered if there was some sort of mother/daughter rivalry cooking in the Hightower kitchen. But after Mrs. Hightower explained that *Carousel* was the only musical The Colorado School for Young Ladies ever puts on, I realized that it would be difficult to prove a mother/daughter rivalry when Bizarro was running the theater department. If *Carousel* was the only musical in town, saints preserve us, it made sense that the two of them might end up in the same role.

I had heard Alicia sing, although not blaring from the edge of a stage, and she seemed to have a nice voice, but the question that nagged me was whether or not she could act. I had known a few actresses in college, had heard stories about the dazzling exhilaration that comes from performing in front of a live audience, and I could see how it might turn the head of a young girl. It's probably similar to receiving an acceptance slip, but I wouldn't know.

Could Alicia act? Admittedly I knew very little about theater life on the whole, but I suspected that the ability to act played a key role in becoming an actress.

It was this thought that gave me a glimmering of an idea that I felt just might help put my conscience to rest. Not forever—just with the Hightower business.

When I woke up the next morning I looked around and discovered that the idea was still in bed with me, which indicated it was probably a serious relationship. I couldn't begin to describe to you all the golden ideas I've had at three o'clock in the morning that either turned to lead overnight or simply climbed out the window while I was snoring. Not enough, believe me. Most of the ideas I've gotten for novels or screenplays have occurred to me while I was either shaving or taking a bath. A number have occurred to me while I was driving 127. I rarely get ideas when seated in front of my typewriter, which I find ironic because I have always suspected that typing somehow plays a key role in writing.

I cooked a hamburger and drank a Coke and watched a little bit of Sunday TV, which thanks to cable, was no different from weekday TV. When I was a kid in Wichita, Sunday morning TV was a living hell. We could watch only three broadcast channels, a show called *Meet the Press,* and no cartoons. Need I say more?

I waited until one P.M. before I made the phone call. I didn't want to make that phone call. I never want to make any phone calls, except to the pizza joint, but this call was particularly abhorrent to me because I was violating a vow that I had made countless times since I had become a cab driver: never get involved in the personal lives of your fares.

"This the Hightower residence ... I cannot come to the phone right now but if you would care to leave your name and phone number I will get back to you as soon as possible beep."

I fought my right arm. I hate answering machines, which is ironic since I also hate talking to people. I don't know why I'm even on the earth.

"Mr. Hightower, this is Murph the taxi driver?"

That was how I talked to the answering machine—with question/statements.

"I hope I'm not disturbing you? The reason I'm calling? I was wondering if I could discuss something with you? It's about your daughter Alicia?"

How in the hell does a person have a conversation with a thing? I kept waiting for the machine to say, "Okay," but it wouldn't. It was like an angry dispatcher giving me the "silent" treatment.

"I'll be around my apartment for the rest of the day? If you would like to call me back I'll be here?"

I couldn't stop this insanity.

I finally garbled some sort of goodbye that I can't recall, and set the receiver on its cradle. My heart was pounding. I was breathing heavily. I stepped toward my chair and the phone rang. I jumped a mile. I don't care what the creative-writing teachers say about clichés—that's exactly how high I jumped: a mile.

I grabbed the receiver off the cradle. "Hello?"

"Murph?"

"Yes?"

Questions, always questions. I hate talking period.

"This is Randolph Hightower. I'm sorry I didn't get to the phone before you hung up. I was doing things."

Doing things is second on my list.

"You said something about Alicia?" he said.

"Yes sir. I wanted to tell you that I ... uh ... I still feel badly about the situation with Alicia and ... uh ... I was wondering if you had heard from her yet?"

He sighed. "No we haven't."

"Well ... uh ... I had an idea that I thought, I don't know, I thought maybe you would like to discuss with me. It has to do with convincing Alicia to leave the film ranch and return to her apartment. And I was just wondering if you would like to get together some time this week so I could tell you my idea."

"How soon can you get over here?" he said.

"Uh …"

The wonderful word "uh." I think of it as "the thought collector."

"Or better yet, why don't I send Jeffrey to pick you up?" he said. "Let's do that."

"Okay."

Jaysus. This guy was a ball of fire. I get nervous around decisive people. They're way out of my league.

Jeffrey asked if I wanted to hear any music. I told him no. We were back in the four-wheel drive but there was no snow on the ground. There was liquor in the cabinet but I didn't touch it. I had ten minutes to get my thoughts together. The reason I hadn't called Hightower until one in the afternoon was because I didn't know if Mrs. Hightower would be awake. This was a Sunday. For a lot of people who drink, there's no such thing as a Sunday morning, and I wanted to give her a chance to be in on this.

When we arrived at the automatic garage door, I knew what I wanted to say. Hightower's obvious willingness to hear me out made it a lot easier on me because I was going to ask him to do something that was going to cost him.

Jeffrey escorted me as far as the library, but didn't step inside with me. Hightower was sitting by the fireplace, but he didn't have a drink in his hand. He was staring at the ashes. Mrs. Hightower wasn't there.

"Good afternoon, Mr. Hightower," I said.

He got out of his chair and smiled. "I think we've reached a point where you can call me Randolph," he said, reaching out to shake my hand.

It was only at this moment that I realized we were close to the same age. It simply hadn't struck me until then. I'm sure he was a little older than me—God knows, he may have been younger, but I never asked. On the inside I've always felt that I was about twenty-two, the age I was when I entered college on the GI Bill. Maybe a nickel psychologist could tell me what that's all about. But there was something about Hightower's wealth, his house, his diction, his sweater, that made me think he was a lot older than me.

"All right, Randolph," I said, shaking his hand.

"Have a seat, Murph."

I sat on the same chair I'd sat on the last two times I'd been there, only now I was sitting on the edge of it.

"Is Mrs. Hightower available?" I said. "I thought she might want to hear this."

He shook his head no. "She's not ... available right now."

I moved on quickly. "Can Alicia act?"

Hightower looked at me querulously. Then he shrugged and said, "She had a lead role in *Carousel* in high school."

"That's what I've been told. But can she act?"

He smiled a kind of sad proud wistful father smile. "I thought she did fine in *Carousel.*"

I nodded, then smiled. "That's understandable. But do you think the critics will be as kind to her as you are?"

He opened his mouth to reply, then closed it and sighed through his nose. He raised his right hand slightly with the fingers spread and shook his head. "Acting is something she claims she wants to do. I think it's foolish. My wife and I want Alicia to go to college. I don't know anything about acting. My wife and I go to plays now and then ..."

He stopped and got a thoughtful look in his eye, then shook his head no and said, "Of course she can't act. She's had no training beyond a lead role in a high school play. None of those kids could act any better than any other group of high school kids. The audience was made up of parents. All of us were proud and entertained, but I don't think there was a serious critic in the house that night."

"Mr. Hightower," I said, then said, "Randolph ... why don't you give your daughter a chance to act?"

"What do you mean?"

"Why don't you fund Toby Brown's next movie and let Alicia find out for herself whether she can act?"

I've read a lot of books and I've seen a lot of movies, and right at that moment I was willing to bet Randolph Hightower had read and seen the same books and movies because he got a look on his face that I've seen in movies and read about in books, a look that I've seen in real life, too, mostly down at Sweeney's Tavern when I'm tapped out and cadging drinks: the word "affronted" leaps to the fore. I was in a rich man's house, talking about spending his money.

When he spoke, a brand-new tone entered his voice and it was not at all congenial. My Univac recognized it. He was beginning to retreat from me verbally.

"I would not give Tobias Brown one thin dime," he said. Apparently clichés didn't bother him. In my experience, businessmen were utterly indifferent to creative writing teachers.

"I'm not talking about giving him a handout," I said. "I'm talking about making an investment that will bring your daughter home."

He began shaking his head no, and raised his right hand as if to ward off any more suggestions from me. But he didn't say anything. His mouth was open, but he didn't talk.

"Screen test," I said.

He slowly lowered his hand.

"I'm not talking about funding some sort of avant-garde nonsense that'll be squeezed into next year's film festival, and I'm sure as hell not talking about doing a feature film. I'm talking about putting up some money to do a demo reel of sorts that will require Alicia to put on an authentic performance that just might tell her what you and your wife have been trying to tell her ever since Alicia got it into her head that a star was born in this house."

He raised his chin slightly, and again looked at me querulously, only this time my Univac spat out the word "intrigued" rather than "disgusted."

"I've been driving a taxi for fourteen years, Randolph, and if there's one thing I've learned it's that sometimes I can't explain to fares that I know a better route to their destination than they do. Sometimes they insist on going the long way even though I know a shorter way. They always think I'm 'up to something.' They think I'm trying to take them on the scenic route. And guess what? When we do it their way we always end up taking the scenic route. I don't know much about daughters, Randolph, but I do know something about hardheaded customers who think they know better than I do. The fact is, sometimes I just have to let my fares do stupid things before they realize how stupid they are. I think you should let Alicia take a ride on the scenic route."

That was a risky thing to say to a man concerning his daughter, but cab driving is a risky business. I wasn't a rich man, but I was a working man who knew his business, and I suspected that Randolph Hightower had gotten to his station in life by knowing when to keep his mouth shut and pay attention to people who knew their business. And right at that moment I was the only asphalt warrior in the room.

CHAPTER 17

I fired up the heap. It was four o'clock on Sunday afternoon and I was headed out to Antoine Baroni's film ranch for the second time in my life, armed with a check and a "plan," as I call certain things.

I figured that this was a good hour of the day to drop in unannounced, for the same reason that I had waited until after lunch to phone the Hightower mansion. If Toby Brown was anything like the filmmakers, writers, and artists that I had known in college, he would be crawling out of the sack about now. There is no such thing as a Sunday morning to lots of people in this world, and there are lots of artists. My own Sunday mornings disappeared when I got drafted and reappeared after I graduated from college.

It was the middle of January, so the days were getting a fraction of a degree longer, but the sun was dipping toward the horizon by the time I pulled into the dirt driveway that led to the house where Toby Brown spent his time and inheritance planning movies. According to Hightower, Toby did not have a job. He lived off the stipend handed to him each month by his father's bankers and lawyers and tax attorneys and whoever else managed to sink their legal fangs into the nest egg that throbbed with financial life. How I envied them.

I drove slowly along the driveway. I could hear dirt clods crumbling beneath my tires. There was no activity outside the house. I could not see any lights on yet, not in the big house and not in the cottage. The scene reminded me of *The Night of the Living Dead* but in a good way. I stopped my heap adjacent to the screened porch. I thought about honking, then decided against it. If anybody was sleeping off a hangover I wasn't about to interrupt it with the blare of a car horn, although I was willing to knock on the door. I call this "compassionate intrusion."

But it wasn't necessary. I saw the front door of the house open. I saw Toby step out onto the screened porch with his hands in his pockets. He was peering at my heap. No way of recognizing my Chevy. I wondered if he kept guns in the house. This had been a working ranch at one time. Ever since the first settlers had arrived in Colorado, ranchers had kept firearms around for shooting snakes, wildcats, and communists, so I imagined Toby's father had owned a few personal sidearms. I decided to roll down my window to let Toby have a good look at me.

He came to the screen door and stared down at me, then lifted a hand out of his pocket and shoved the door open. He moved down the steps at a slow pace, nodded at me, gave up a small smile, and said, "Hi Murph. What brings you out here?" He seemed laconic but not hung over. I can spot a hangover a mile away. I'm third-generation Irish-Catholic.

"I came here to get Alicia," I said.

He froze.

It was as if I had uttered a magic incantation. I sensed hope radiating from him—the hippies used to call it "vibes" although I doubt if they invented the word. I once ran across the phrase "outa sight" in *Maggie* by Stephen Crane, which was written in the nineteenth century. I don't know why I bring that up.

Toby shook his head no. "I don't think she wants to leave," he said, glancing over at the cottage.

"Is she asleep?" I said.

"Yeah. She's sleeping one off."

"Good," I said. "Because you and I need to talk."

He looked down at his sandaled feet, kicked at a dirt clod and said, "If you were planning to make her get into your car and drive her back to Denver, it won't work. I spent most of yesterday trying to get her to leave and she won't go."

"Was she drinking when you talked to her about it?" I said.

"No."

"Well there's your problem. It's impossible to reason with sober people."

He squinted at me. I knew he couldn't tell whether or not I was kidding. That made two of us. "But I didn't come here to try and talk her into leaving," I said. "I came here to try and talk you into making a movie."

His demeanor changed. My Univac picked up on it fast. I imagined that Toby had been approached by a lot of people who wanted him to make a movie. I myself had been approached by people who tried to talk me into writing things after they learned I was an aspiring writer—gratis of course. People have a peculiar attitude toward writers. They think writers are desperate to write things for free out of the goodness of their altruistic hearts. I blame early twentieth-century social-realists for this, primarily Upton Sinclair. But to get back to the point, a new vibe began emanating from Toby. My Univac spat out the word "wary." I moved fast.

"This involves the production of a short film. I already have the money to produce it," I said. I assumed there wasn't much difference between writers and filmmakers, which was why I uttered the magic word "money." It's as universal as Yellow Cab hats.

Two minutes later I was sitting at the kitchen table inside Toby's ranch house. He placed a can of beer in front of me and sat down with his own beer.

"Ever since I made the mistake of bringing Alicia out here I haven't been able to get into the cottage to do any work," he said. "That's where I keep all my film equipment. It's where I do my editing. Not that it matters now."

I took a sip of beer. "You were going to use that twelve hundred to finance a movie, weren't you?" I said. I wanted this out in the open. If anybody was going to be playing cute games from now on, I wanted it to be me.

He nodded.

"How can you produce a movie for twelve hundred dollars?" I said.

He smiled. "Well ... one way you can do it is to not pay your crew."

"Makes sense," I said. "But that probably wouldn't work in Hollywood."

"I'm not interested in Hollywood," he said. "I'm interested in making movies."

That zinger was so subtle that it almost got past me. I grinned as it brushed an earlobe.

"I own all of my own equipment," he said. "I don't have to rent anything. But raw film stock costs money, and then there's the developing and the distribution." He shrugged. "There's expenses."

I nodded. I thought about novel writing. A sheaf of blank paper and a typewriter ribbon cost money, too, but buying them is the easy part. The hard part is writing the novel. Publishers always leave the hard part up to the people with no money.

"How long have you been making movies?" I said.

"Since I was a kid," he said. "My father gave me an eight-millimeter movie camera. I horsed around with it all through high school but never did anything serious. I went off to college and took a few film theory courses and a couple filmmaking classes but I didn't get serious about it until after I graduated."

"What was your major?" I said, then braced myself to hear the word "English." I probably run into more English majors than any cabbie in Colorado.

"Pre-med," he said.

I heaved an internal sigh of relief.

He picked up his beer and took a sip, then set it down. "My father wanted me to become a veterinarian. I made it as far as my junior year before I realized I would never be a vet. I switched my major to theater, and my father practically disowned me."

I worked hard to keep from showing any expression. Things began to make sense, which was a new one on me. I had wondered why his father stipulated in his will that Toby receive a pittance until he turned thirty. Now I knew: send the kid out into the real world and give him ten years to learn the hard way how difficult it is to make a living when your career is anchored by an elusive dream. My Maw would have made a good rancher.

I took a long drink of beer and set the can down. "There won't be any problem with expenses on this movie," I said. "The finances are all taken care of."

"Are you planning to finance it yourself?" he said.

I had long ago noticed that whenever money is discussed by human beings, a third party always seems to join the conversation. His presence is felt even if his body is invisible. For lack of a better name I call him "Tippy"—not to be confused with Tippi Hedren. People seem to tiptoe around each other until money issues are resolved one way or another. I could feel Tippy now. We were discussing the financing of a project that had not yet been described. This made sense to me, and indicated that Toby Brown was tiptoeing on familiar ground. Inexperienced artists usually save money talk for last, often in bankruptcy court.

"No," I said. "I'm not financing this project. Randolph Hightower is financing it. Alicia's father. He wants a screen test. He wants to find out whether or not Alicia can really act." The distance began to shrink. I could see it in Toby's eyes. "Mr. Hightower has given me ten thousand dollars to put together a short reel."

The distance was gone. Toby raised his beer to his lips and listened just like Mr. Hightower had listened. Toby may have been a broke filmmaker but I could tell he knew his business, too.

"Mr. Hightower left the scripting of the demo reel up to us. The idea is that you put Alicia through her paces as an actress. You take her to the edge—whatever the hell the edge amounts to in a screen test. But here's the caveat. Alicia has to go back to her apartment. We'll be shooting the screen test in downtown Denver. We're going to rent a space for a week or so. You're going to have to explain to her that she'll need to move back to her apartment so she can be available every morning at six A.M."

I looked him in the eye when I said this. I wasn't sure how the phrase "six A.M." would affect him. "Noon" is the crack-of-doom for artists.

He didn't bat an eye.

"As far as the financing goes, Alicia doesn't have to know where the money is coming from," I said. "As far as she knows, the money is mine. Seed money. As far as she knows, you and I are trying to put together a demo reel that we're going to take to a group of dentists looking to finance a motion picture. Grade B. But we'll tell her that there are no promises. It's a gamble. It may come to nothing. She has to understand this. She also has to understand that you're the one who talked me into giving her the screen test. I was reluctant. She doesn't have a film résumé. I don't know if she can act. But you convinced me. I'm putting up ten grand to find out whether she's got what it takes to go straight to video."

Toby didn't interrupt me once. I liked that.

"The way I see it," I continued, "you just might be able to convince Alicia to go home this evening. I'll drive her. All you have to do is go over to that cottage and make your pitch."

Toby took another drink, then set the can on the table.

"When do we start shooting?" he said.

"As soon as I write the script."

He smiled. I smiled back. Isn't this how they do it out in Hollywood—put together a package, a star, a director, a crew, and then start looking around for a script? That's how Roger Corman shot *The Little Shop of Horrors*, didn't he? I hope so. I would hate to think he planned it.

"One other thing," I said. "Mr. Hightower doesn't want Alicia to become an actress. He wants Alicia to fail the test. If I let you do the edit alone, you'd probably do a good job, but if I oversee the final cut, the movie is guaranteed to nosedive."

He smiled at that, but then the smile faded as he looked down at his beer. He didn't say anything. I could tell he was thinking it over.

"Alicia has to go home," I said. "She's just a kid."

He took a deep breath and sighed, then looked up at a clock on the wall above the fridge. It was almost five. Toby began nodding. He scooted his chair back from the table and said, "I'll go wake her up."

When they came into the kitchen Alicia was wearing her flapper dress and a smile. The dress was clean. She'd had a week to clean it. I'm talking a "drinker's week." The standard seven days are completely arbitrary in a drinker's week and are measured by a minimum of one minor accomplishment, as well I know.

"Alicia, this is Murph." Toby said. He was all smiles, too.

"We've met," she said. She was being cute, like she had been cute that night a week earlier when she'd been drunk. She wasn't drunk now. "Toby told me all about the film project," she said. "Thanks for inviting me to be a part of it."

"Well, on the night we met, you told me you were an actress," I said. "So I figured what the heck, let's go ahead and give you a screen test."

The room was full of actors that night.

We sat at the kitchen table for a few minutes while I explained things to her. The dentists. The demo reel. The mercurial nature of show-biz. She ate it up. I winked at her and said, "I think you've got what it takes, Babycakes," even though I knew I was toying with a horsewhipping.

She agreed to let me drive her back to Denver. I had brought an extra coat for the ride. As we stepped outside to get into my heap, Toby said goodbye. I could tell he was pleased to the point of giddiness. In fact, I could not recall ever having gotten a goodbye as enthusiastic as the one I received from Toby that evening, which is saying a lot because most people are absolutely ecstatic when I go away.

CHAPTER 18

Things were back to normal. Alicia was living in her apartment again and the preproduction activities for the demo reel were in the hands of Toby Brown, alias Antoine Baroni. All I had to do was come up with an idea for a screenplay.

On Monday morning I picked up 127 at the motor, then drove to the nearest 7-11 and gassed up, bought a Coke and a Twinkie, and drove downtown to find a place in the cab line at the Brown Palace. There were only three cabs ahead of me. The sky was clear but the air was cold, so I sat with my windows rolled up, the engine idling, and the heater blowing while I did brunch.

After I had dropped Alicia off at her apartment on Sunday night I drove back to my crow's nest and spent a demoralizing evening sifting through my classic collection of unsold screenplays before I finally concluded that I would have to come up with an original concept. Being an unpublished writer I had naturally gone with my first instinct, which was to cannibalize something I hadn't been able to palm off on a studio. But it was only when I began to think of my screenplays as being actually turned into films that I realized why no studio had ever shown the slightest interest in them.

It's a funny thing about writing. You get so balled up in a story idea that you lose your perspective and forget that human beings might read your words someday. As I sat there trying to choose one of my scripts as a basis for a film project, I found myself saying, "Who wrote this stuff?" followed by the inevitable question, "Did he actually believe someone was going to give him money?"

The cabs moved forward one space every five minutes. I sat staring out the windshield trying to come up with a thirty-minute concept that would showcase Alicia Hightower's talents, or lack thereof. But there was one thing I had already decided on, and that was a singing bit. Whether or not she would prove to be the equal of Shirley Jones, she would be given a fair shot.

Then I was first in line at the Brown and I put show-biz out of my mind. "Cherry Creek Shopping Center," a businessman said as he climbed into the rear of my cab. I figured he was good for ten bucks. Murph the producer/cabbie was back on the road.

When I dropped him off in front of the main entrance to the mall there were no other cabs in the queue, but there was a woman waiting for a ride. The doorman who runs the valet service flagged me down, so I caught another ten-dollar trip that took me over to east Sixth Avenue. I had to carry the woman's sacks from Saks as far as the front door. When I got back into 127, I turned on the radio as I always do when there are no hotels nearby, and I jumped a bell on east Colfax.

A middle-aged black woman was waiting at the curb near a telephone booth. I pulled up, and as soon as she climbed in she bellowed, "The cure for cancer is in the earth!" I nodded politely and asked for an address. She gave me a number three miles farther east on Colfax, then she said again, "The cure for cancer is in the earth!"

It's always difficult to respond to statements like that, so I just let it ride and hoped the conversation would work itself out.

"Do you believe that?" the woman said.

"I suppose it is, ma'am," I said, and I gave the accelerator a little extra toe. I did not have a clue as to what she was talking about. It was a typical taxi Monday.

But then she said, "It resides in a leaf, or in a root, or in an herb. The good Lord put the cure for every single disease somewhere in the earth, and our job is to find it. That's what we were put here to do. The cure for cancer is in the earth!"

Suddenly we were on the same wavelength. I understood what she was talking about. I pulled up at the address, and it turned out to be an herb shop in a little storefront. The meter read six dollars and she gave me seven. "God bless you," she said when she climbed out. I always feel embarrassed when people say that to me. I haven't been to church since I left Wichita, but that's just between you and me—my Maw doesn't have a "need to know."

I made fifty dollars that day, my standard profit-taking, and when I got back to my crow's nest a little after seven, I called Toby just to "touch bases." Now that I was a producer/cabbie and not just a regular/cabbie I was trying to work as much show-biz jargon into my schmooze as possible. Toby told me he had found a space in LoDo that we could rent for a week to do the shoot. Then he asked me how the screenplay was coming.

Strangely enough I broke into a sweat. I felt the way I used to feel when I worked for Dyna-Plex. It had been fourteen years since I had found myself writing under a deadline, and it was like a recurrence of Yellow Fever. They made me wear a white shirt and a tie at Dyna-Plex. Pants, too. I was a corporate writer and once a month I had a deadline to beat.

My basic job was to write a brochure for the corporation, even though to this day I do not have a clue as to what Dyna-Plex produced or manufactured or serviced or whatever corporations do. I don't even know what the word "corporation" means, and I love words. I would spend twenty-nine days doing nothing, and then on the thirtieth day I would take an hour in the morning and write a thousand words and hand it in to my boss. That was the text for the brochure. But during that hour I felt like Atlas being crushed under the weight of the world because I didn't have any idea what I was writing about. I had to make it up. It was like writing a novel, especially the thousand-words-a-month part.

One day I killed some time figuring out that there are 8,760 hours in a single year. It didn't take long to figure that out because I used a pocket calculator. During my year at Dyna-Plex I had spent twelve of those hours on the brochure, and it nearly broke me as a man. I use the word "nearly" because I can't think of another word that comes closer than "nearly."

I told Toby that I was making "headway" on the script.

"Let me know what you come up with," he said.

"Will do," I said.

I almost said, "Roger that." I used to say that in the army a lot. I didn't like saying it, but if I didn't say it the other soldiers would look at me funny, so I conformed. I just wanted to put in my two years of service and get out with my vocabulary intact.

I called Randolph Hightower then. I wanted to "touch bases" with him, too, since he was paying for the shoot. After I brought him "up-to-date" I hung up the phone and spent a minute trying to think of who else I could "touch bases" with. I was getting to like "touching bases." It made me feel important. But I couldn't think of anyone else to call. Like most cab drivers I don't have many friends, and of the people that I do know, none of them want me touching anything while I'm talking to them.

I spent the rest of the evening contemplating scenes that could be acted out by Alicia Hightower, but the word "deadline" kept getting in the way. I couldn't concentrate. I had a check for ten thousand dollars that I was going to deposit in the bank on Tuesday morning, I had a director scouting locations, an actress waiting for a script, and a full-blown case of writer's block. I felt like a pro.

Then I had an inspiration. I picked up the phone and called an actress that I had known in college. Her name was Mitzy. She had been waiting tables at Sweeney's Tavern for a long time, and had appeared in community theater productions. She was at Sweeney's that night. After I got her on the phone I told her I was putting together a demo reel and wanted to know what sort of things actresses did during auditions. She asked me why the hell I hadn't invited her to try out for the part. The conversation was barely thirty seconds old and was already disintegrating. I thought fast. "The actress we're auditioning is the executive producer's daughter," I said.

"Gotcha," she said.

She winked, I'm sure of it.

She told me there were plenty of books at the library filled with practice scenes from plays and movies that could be used for an audition. Then Sweeney asked her politely how soon she might be finished talking on the phone. I could hear his charming Irish brogue in the background. She told him she was talking to Murph, and he told her to hang the hell up.

The next morning I went to the bank and deposited the check in my account, then drove over to the Denver Public Library and began looking for practice play books. They had plenty. It was like the section on how-to books for novelists. Stacks of them. I sometimes get the feeling there are more people who know how to do things than actually do them.

The books contained scenes which ran the gamut from Shakespeare to Sam Shepherd, but I picked out a couple books focusing on twentieth-century theater—Eugene O'Neill, George S. Kaufman, etc., figuring that a girl who had never read a novel was going to have enough trouble memorizing her lines without having to deal with "zounds."

At noon Toby and I "did lunch" at a McDonald's. We "did" two hamburgers each, and afterward I "did" a smuggled Twinkie. He satisfied himself with "doing" a cup of coffee while I explained that because time was short I had decided to forego writing an original screenplay and just run with a few established works of art. He almost fouled me up when he asked what I meant by saying "time was short." In fact, we had all the time in the world, but I was so swept up in the excitement of avoiding writing a screenplay that it didn't occur to me that he might question my lame excuse. This was the first time I had ever collaborated with someone on avoiding writing. I usually avoid writing on my own.

"I only meant that Mr. Hightower will probably want this shoot completed as soon as possible," I said. "We don't have a deadline, but I figured why put a lot of work into a new screenplay when we can use material written by someone else."

I showed him the books. He leafed through them, then said he would be happy to pick a few things out for Alicia to practice. I told him it was fine with me, to do whatever he wanted, that I preferred he take charge of the whole show since I had no experience whatsoever with shooting a movie.

I could tell he was glad of that, and not only because I could see it in his eyes but because he said so. He said that one reason he wanted to become an independent producer was to avoid the sort of interference that you traditionally see in Hollywood, where producers think they're writers. I knew what he meant. The delusion that you're a writer is the province of cabbies.

After lunch we drove down to LoDo. Toby showed me the space he wanted to rent for the shoot. It was in a warehouse not far from the gallery where all this had started, sort of. It was a four-story red brick building that we could lease at two thousand dollars for five days. The ground floor was a gigantic hollow space. It was like a sound stage in the movies. Walking around inside the hollow shell of what would become the studio for the demo reel reminded me of the six months I had lived in Los Angeles before I came to Denver. I wrote an unsold screenplay when I was there. I supported myself with a job delivering designer ice cream to restaurants all over the LA basin. I eventually got fired. That's how most of my stories end.

Toby said he was going to use the same crew that I had met on Wednesday. I asked him if they would even consider working for him after that fracas, but he said they were a good crew and got surly only when they didn't get paid. I knew the feeling. Whenever one of my fares leapt out of the backseat at a stoplight and ran away without paying, I would get surly. But I stopped chasing fares on foot thirteen years ago. One day I caught up with an escaped fare. After I grabbed him, his false teeth fell out and he started beating me with his cane. God knows how things would have turned out if that cop hadn't come along and arrested me.

CHAPTER 19

By turning everything except the final edit of the demo reel over to Toby, I had, in a sense, washed my hands of the Hightower Affair. From my point of view, the unfinished trip on the night of the Gatsby party was completed and I could get on with my vow of never again getting involved in the personal lives of my fares. My conscience was as salved as my conscience ever gets. Alicia Hightower was going to get her screen test, shot by a filmmaker who was as close to a pro as I knew personally, which was a mighty slim pick. Whether or not she could act, or be convinced she couldn't act, Director Antoine Baroni was going to put her through her paces.

I'll admit it. I felt smug. I had figured out another way to get rid of guilt feelings, something I had been good at ever since my first confession at Blessed Virgin Catholic Church. Whether it involved cussing behind the rectory, swiping a pack of chewing gum from the local Ben Franklin store, or eyeballing a *Playboy* at the Rexall, all I had to do was make a quick trip to the confessional, say a few Hail Marys, and bingo, I was set for another week of sin. After I left Wichita I got even better at it.

My ability to avoid guilt feelings also stood me in good stead in the army where I dodged more details than any yardbird in the history of mops. Don't ask me how I got an honorable discharge. There must have been a mix-up at the Pentagon. Sometimes it takes more work to avoid guilt than it takes to avoid work. But that's because with work all you have to do is walk away from a job. But how do you walk away from your conscience? Trust me, I'm working on it.

When I woke up on Wednesday morning I felt like a free man. I drove my heap down to Rocky, picked up my key and trip-sheet from Rollo, and even managed to smile at the sonofabitch. He gave me a suspicious look and said, "Did you kill that girl?" Things were back to normal.

I headed for 7-11 to take care of gas and Twinkies, then drove straight to the Brown Palace and got in line. I turned off the Rocky radio, turned on the AM, unwrapped my snack and picked up my paperback. Twenty minutes later I was first in line in the queue. A man came out of the Brown carrying a suitcase, got into the rear of 127, and said the magic acronym, "DIA." Fifty bucks guaranteed.

After I dropped him off, I cruised past the staging area where sixty or so cabs were parked waiting for a miracle. I laughed and deadheaded back to Denver. Life couldn't have been sweeter.

Toby had told me that I was welcome to drop by the "studio" any time to see how the shoot was coming along. This was the exact opposite of the way things worked in Hollywood, or so I've read in the hundreds of books on film lore that I've bought during the past fifteen years.

I can't speak from personal experience and probably never will, but from what I understand, the screenwriter is the last person a director wants to see on a sound stage during the filming of a movie. After the director has those one hundred and twenty pages of pure gold in his hand, he doesn't want to hear from the wunderkind who figured out how to write, pad, chop, carve, and stretch a thin premise into two hours of dynamite entertainment. But I do empathize. I wouldn't want a pump jockey telling me how to gouge fares.

But I lied and told Toby I would be driving all week and wouldn't be able to drop in. I knew I would eventually have to help edit the demo reel, but I wasn't looking forward to it. If Alicia couldn't act, I did not especially relish the idea of being there when she found out. I've had plenty of experience discovering that I couldn't do things, and while I myself am used to it, she was just a kid. Youth is a tough gig, which is why I'm always sympathetic to teenagers and always try to play straight with them when they make the mistake of asking me for advice. I tell them things they don't want to hear, like study hard, stay off drugs, and don't run away from home—and if all else fails, act mature.

But I always feel badly telling kids to try and be as grownup as possible because a lot of young people seem to have the impression that adulthood is an eternal rock concert. Just because my life is like that doesn't mean theirs will be anything except low-paying jobs, unwanted responsibilities, and chronic nostalgia. I try to break it to them gently. I tell them that youth officially ends when they turn eighteen unless they go to college, in which case they get an extension of four years to act like morons. I myself dragged it out to seven years, but I was financed by the federal government—GI Bill money—and believe me, when drunken sailors start throwing money at drunken soldiers, turn out the lights and call the cops. Mainly though, I try to convince kids to learn as much as possible. I tell them that it all ties in with this unpleasant concept known as "self-reliance."

"Like it or not, you're going to have to start taking personal responsibility for your own actions someday," I say to them. "So you might as well start learning how to do it now. I know it sounds awful, but wait until you're an adult. It gets even worse, but the pay is great."

I had a pretty good Friday. I grossed eighty bucks. Storm clouds had started coming in from the west during the last hour of my shift, so I was glad that my week of driving was over even if it did look like snow. This was the exact opposite of how I normally respond to bad weather. As I said, we cabbies refer to snow as "white gold" and there had been plenty of times when I was tempted to drive on a Saturday because of snow— but only tempted. Having been raised Catholic, I was familiar with the ins-and-outs of fighting temptation. I had never applied that knowledge to sin—but work? That was another story. I recognize the tools of the devil when he casts them in my path in order to trip me up—profits, prestige, fame—I see them for what they really are. Whenever Satan tries to entice me with the siren song of work, I just whisper a few Hail Marys and drag the blanket over my head.

That's what I got busy doing as soon as I woke up on Saturday morning. I peeked out the window and saw more than an inch of snow on the ground—an inch of pure gold as far as I was concerned. The old electric thrill shot through me, a sensation that might have been experienced by a Yukon sourdough eyeballing a *Playboy*.

But I fought it. I had that blanket over my eyes in a trice. I thought I heard the devil stamping his feet with rage out in the storm so I lifted the pillow off my face just to check, and it turned out to be the phone ringing.

At any other time I would have let it ring until the person at the other end gave up and removed himself from my life forever. But this had been The Week Of The Rings, so I knew I had better answer it.

I staggered into the living room and picked up the receiver.

"Hello?"

It was at this moment that I realized I raise my eyebrows when I say hello.

"Murph?"

"Yes?"

"This is Toby."

"What's going on?" I said, slipping a real question into the exchange.

"I'm down at the studio in LoDo. Listen … uh … have you heard from Alicia?"

"What do you mean … this morning?"

"Yeah."

"No. I haven't spoken to Alicia since I drove her home from your ranch last Sunday."

There was an ominous silence at the other end of the line. I suddenly felt like I was driving 127 with a really strange person in the backseat. As I say, silence in a taxi can be unnerving.

"So what's up?" I said.

"There's something funny going on," Toby said. I closed my eyes and sighed.

Telephones.

"Define 'funny,'" I croaked.

"Well ... we finished most of the shoot and I've been looking at a lot of developed footage for the past couple days. Dailies, you know. I spliced a lot of shots together but it wasn't really edited. I was supposed to meet Alicia here this morning to start working on the final edit, only she never showed up."

"What time is it right now?" I said.

"Eleven."

"Have you tried calling her apartment?"

"Yes, but nobody answers."

I nodded. I didn't care if he couldn't see me. Is there some rule that says you can't nod when nobody sees it?

"Well ... can't you do the edit without her?" I said.

"That's another funny thing," Toby said. "I can't find the film."

Suddenly I was wide awake. "What do you mean?"

"The dailies that we've been looking at, they're gone."

"Like stolen?"

"No. Not exactly. It's more like someone with a key got in here last night and took them without my permission."

"Does Alicia have a key?"

"Yes."

I was going to ask why she had a key, but decided not to bother. I've never been heavily into finger pointing, since most fingers point at me.

"Do you think she took the film?" I said.

"Yes. I mean, I can't imagine a crew member taking the film."

"Wait a minute ... wait a minute ... they've been paid, haven't they?"

"Yes."

Whew. I backtracked on that angle. "So you think Alicia came in last night and took the film?"

"Yes."

"Why would she do that?"

"I have no idea," Toby said. "Maybe she's up to something."

That hit me like a ton of bricks. Alicia Hightower was eighteen years old and a citizen of the United States. Of course she was up to something.

I started to feel dizzy.

"Listen Toby, let me get back to you," I said. "I'll see what I can find out. Maybe her father knows where she is."

"All right. I'll be here at the studio."

We rang off.

I went back to my bedroom and fell face forward onto my mattress. This is how I respond to everything that happens to me, so there was nothing unusual about it.

I decided I had to find Alicia. Of the ten thousand dollars that Mr. Hightower gave me, we had spent nearly seven thousand already on the studio, crew salaries, raw film stock, and box lunches. The demo reel was nearly completed, but we didn't have any footage to show for it. Ergo, I wasn't about to contact Randolph Hightower.

I got dressed and ate a quick cheese sandwich, washed it down with a Coke, and headed into the storm. There were two inches of snow on the ground. I could hear the devil laughing, but I had the poor sap fooled. I wasn't going to work. I was going to an address on east 14th Avenue.

I had no trouble finding the place. I had been there twice, although on the other two occasions it was dark and Alicia Hightower was either getting into my vehicle or getting out. I parked around the corner and walked to the front of the apartment building. I entered the foyer and looked at a row of doorbells. There were no names next to the buttons, but it didn't matter because I knew which apartment Alicia lived in. The Rocky dispatcher had given me the number the first time I had met

Alicia. I pressed it and waited for either the door to buzz or a voice to come over the speaker. The speaker spoke.

"Yes?"

"This is Murph the taxi driver. Am I speaking to Alicia?"

"No."

"Is she there?"

"No."

"Do you know where she is?"

"Yes."

"Can you tell me?"

"No."

"Why not?"

"She asked me not to tell anyone where she is."

"Okay," I said. "I'm going to call the police now, and then I'm going to call her father."

"Just a minute," she said.

I wondered if it was the police or the father that changed her mind.

After a minute Alicia's roommate Melanie came to the door. There was a window covered by a lace curtain. Melanie parted the curtain and looked at me.

"Alicia asked me not to tell anyone where she was going."

"If you don't tell me, I'll call the police," I said. "Where did she go?"

"To Hollywood," Melanie said. "She took a flight at six o'clock this morning."

My soul fell right out of my shoes.

CHAPTER 20

My first instinct was to run away. By "first" I mean "only." I have no other instincts that I know of.

By setting up a screen test I had inadvertently caused an eighteen-year-old girl to fly to Hollywood armed with nothing more than a demo reel and a dream.

"What will her father do to me when he finds out?" I asked myself.

How many times had I asked that during the past thirty years? Then Melanie opened the door and said, "You're the taxi driver who brought Alicia home last week, aren't you?"

"Yes."

My entire being became focused on maintaining my cool, which I am good at. After fourteen years of driving a cab and having every sort of geek, cretin, and crackpot in my backseat, I was good at pretending to be nonchalant. My only regret was that I didn't have my squirt bottle of ammonia in my shirt pocket. Maybe I could blind Melanie, race back to my crow's nest, pack a bag, and drive to Wichita. It was only eight hundred miles—I could be there in eight hours. You do the math.

"Alicia told me all about you," Melanie said.

Jaysus. This was getting worse.

"She said you were responsible for helping her to realize her dream. She told me to thank you if you came by."

I started to lose my cool. Had I given Alicia any specific advice? I couldn't remember. Under normal circumstances I give advice to people only if they ask for it—unless it's an emergency, or I'm bored.

"Did you drive her to the airport this morning?" I said.

"No, she took a Yellow Cab." That hurt.

"Did she say why she was going to Los Angeles?"

"She said she had passed the screen test and was going to Hollywood to get a job."

I raised my hand to my forehead and held it for a moment, then lowered it. "Was she drunk when she said this?" I hoped.

"No, but she did seem really happy."

"Did she take anything with her?" I said.

"A suitcase."

"How about a reel of film?"

"I don't know. I didn't see one."

Of course she took one. And I knew where she was headed, too. She would be knocking on the doors of talent agencies. She would be showing her reel to guys who smoked cigars. She would be talking to sleazeballs who would make her promises they couldn't keep and had no intention of anyway. I knew the type. I had lived in Los Angeles for six months. I saw them in bars. I saw them in bistros. I saw them at the Whiskey A-Go-Go. I even talked to one once. I told him I was trying to write a screenplay. He told me to quit trying and just do it. I wasn't sure if he was being sarcastic or helpful. Probably both. It didn't matter. I never finished the screenplay. It was my first effort. I was young. I didn't know that "convoy" movies were out of vogue.

Melanie frowned and said, "You're not really going to call the police are you? Alicia hasn't done anything wrong, has she?"

This confirmed it: Melanie didn't have a clue. That made two of us. But I had no excuse for being clueless. I was a trained professional cab driver. I was an adult, at least in people years. But I didn't know what to do. I didn't want to call Toby and tell him what had happened. I didn't want to call Mr. Hightower. I had a vision of giant fingers pointing at me from every direction. I felt the same way I felt in college whenever I woke up from a binge and couldn't find my pants.

"No, I'm not going to call the police," I told her. I started backing away. "I have to go now. If Alicia calls, say hello for me."

I wanted to return to my crow's nest, dive into bed, and pull the blanket over my face. This always helped me to remember where my pants were, but I had a feeling pants weren't going to solve this problem. When I first started driving a cab, I was advised by my trainer never to get involved in the personal lives of my fares because it just led to trouble. My trainer was a guy named Big Al. "Steer clear of altruism," he told me. "It's riskier than taking personal checks."

I turned and walked away. I didn't feel safe until I got around the corner and out of sight of Melanie, who seemed like a threat to me even though I was the one who had threatened her with the cops. But she had seen me in person. She had told me where Alicia went. She had given me knowledge. I felt like Pandora's Box. But mostly I felt guilt. I don't mean guilty, I mean the short version—the silver bullet—GUILT!

Drive, guilt said.

I started the engine and pulled away from the curb. I must have gone fifteen blocks before I realized where I was. I had driven north across Colfax and was wandering around in an old residential section of Denver. I didn't know where I was going. I was just driving. It was like the time I left Wichita after dropping out of the state university to become a novelist, after my Maw threw me out of the house, after Mary Margaret Flaherty said she wouldn't marry me. I eventually found myself in Atlanta. Not this time, the other time.

For all I knew, Alicia Hightower was already in the clutches of some fly-by-night Tinseltown talent agent. The taxi ride that I had tried to complete by setting up a screen test had taken a wrong turn and was now careening down the boulevard of broken dreams.

I looked at my wristwatch. It was past noon. I turned my heap west. I wanted to go back to my crow's nest but I just kept driving—down The Hill and across Broadway, down into the financial district, down past all the hotels where Yellow Cabs and Rocky Cabs and all the other Denver hacks were idling away their hours waiting for fares to come out of hotels for a ride to DIA.

I looked longingly at the taxis as I drove past. I looked at the cabbies snoring on the front seats or reading newspapers. Their lives were so simple. So easy. You didn't see them getting involved in the personal lives of their fares and delivering innocent young girls into the hands of men with couches. The only cabbie engaged in that enterprise was skulking through downtown Denver looking for the nearest exit from reality.

Actually I was looking for the 15th Street Bridge.

Don't get me wrong. I wasn't planning to take The Big Dive. It was worse than that.

I was going to an off-track betting joint just across the river. I didn't even realize I was going there until I was on the viaduct, but that's where I had been headed ever since saying goodbye to Melanie. My subconscious had taken over the wheel. I was too inept to drive, too inept to give advice, too inept to do anything but curl into a ball on the front seat and cower, which I had been good at ever since I left college. I was going to the off-track betting joint because that's where the only person in the world who could help me spent his Saturdays—my mentor, my conscience, my oracle, my judge, my jury, and my executioner, the man who had trained me to drive a taxi fourteen years earlier: Big Al.

The betting joint was located on the first floor of a nineteenth-century building up the hill from the river. The room was small and crowded. The Colorado tracks were closed for the winter season, but anybody with money to lose could come to the off-track and watch the races from Caliente to Sarasota on closed-circuit TV. I had dropped plenty of fares off at this joint, and had picked up the losers who still had enough scratch to afford one last trip to where their wives lived—some people call it "home." Big Al was seated at his regular table with a clear view of five TVs running different races simultaneously. He was studying a tip-sheet and making notes with a pencil. By "notes" I mean numbers. He was figuring the odds.

I swallowed hard. I didn't want to go up to him and tell him what I had done, but I had nowhere else to turn. I had dropped the ball. I was scared. I was just an ordinary Joe looking for a way out. I approached his table with trepidation. His pencil was wiggling. I hated to interrupt him. Figuring the odds was a sacred ritual to Big Al. Almost as sacred as being left alone. Big Al was the man who had introduced me to dog-track betting a long time ago.

He glanced up to check the tote board, and noticed me standing there.

"Hey Tenderfoot, what's popping?" he said, and looked down at his tip-sheet, but quickly looked back up. "What are you doing here?" he said. "What did I tell you about betting?"

He had told me to stick with cab driving.

"I didn't come here to bet," I said.

He grunted his approval, then looked back down at his tip-sheet. "Did you drop off a fare here?" he said.

When I didn't reply, he glanced up. "Wait a minute. This is Saturday. You don't drive on Saturdays."

I nodded.

"Oh no," Big Al said. He closed his eyes and shook his head. "I recognize that look."

"What look?"

"Don't get coy with me." He set the pencil down and leaned back in his chair. He folded his arms and pointed a finger at the empty chair across from him.

I slid into the seat and ducked my head instinctively.

"You did it again, didn't you, Tenderfoot. What did I tell you about getting involved in the personal lives of your fares?"

Big Al had invented the phrase "cut to the chase."

"I need help," I said.

"How bad?"

"Real bad."

"Do you need money?"

"No."

"Then it's not that bad."

"It's worse than bad."

"How much worse?"

"It's a moral quandary."

He glanced at the tote board. "Can it wait until after the next race?"

"Yes."

Big Al got up from the table and went to make a bet. I looked around the room. It was packed with bettors standing with their heads bowed reading tip-sheets. Nobody was smiling. The floor was littered with tickets. The room looked the way Dante would have described Purgatory if there had been off-track betting in the fourteenth century.

"I want to know as few details as possible," Big Al said when he got back to the table.

I gave it to him straight. I told him it involved an eighteen-year-old girl.

"The girl everybody thought you murdered last week?"

I nodded. What the hell.

"It's a long story," I said.

"Make it short."

"Due to a series of well-intended machinations on my part, she inadvertently ran off to Hollywood to become a movie star."

He gazed at me for a moment, then picked up his pencil and leaned into his trip-sheet. "And you feel that you are to blame."

"Yes."

"I won't argue with that."

"But the thing is …" I started to say.

"No buts," he said. "I don't want details. All I want to know is what you intend to do about the fact that you have undoubtedly ruined another human being's existence."

"I was thinking of moving to Wichita."

"I was going to recommend Pierre, South Dakota."

"I don't know what to do, Big Al. She's probably out there right now getting chewed up and spat out or whatever Hollywood does to eighteen-year-old kids who can't act."

"What's acting got to do with it?" he said. "Did you ever see a beach party movie?"

"I've seen them all," I said.

"Did you ever see anybody who could act in one of those things?"

"Robert Cummings."

"Touché."

He continued to work his pencil, making numbers on his tip-sheet and occasionally glancing at the tote board. But I knew he was paying attention to the issue at hand. Big Al could add multiple numbers in his head while simultaneously jumping bells and reading a map. Sometimes he did that just to make me feel inferior. It worked.

"The horses are running at Del Mar," he said. "Excuse me one moment." He got up from the table and went to a betting window.

When the race started, the inmates of Il Purgatorio came alive and gathered around the TV sets. It was like the scene in *Dog Day Afternoon* when Al Pacino was baiting the crowd and waving his handkerchief. Then it was like the fadeout of *Bonnie and Clyde*. The inmates bowed their heads. Big Al made a quick stop at a window, then came back to the table and sat down.

"Where were we?" he said.

"Her father is a rich man," I said, hoping I wasn't crossing the line on the details angle. Big Al could be touchy about knowing too much about anything. "He isn't aware yet that his daughter left town."

Big Al nodded. He reached into his shirt pocket and pulled out a wad of bills and tossed it in front of me.

"What's this?" I said.

"You have to go get her and bring her back," he said. "You just won that money, compliments of a mudder named Queenie Blue. I put fifty bucks on the nose for you. I figured you'd need it for a quick flight out of town."

"What makes you think I need money?" I said.

"I'll ignore that and move on," he said. "Panic is the tie that binds us. I'll never forget the moment you sat in the driver's seat of my cab on your first day of training and a call came over the radio. I thought you were going to faint."

I'll admit it. When I took my very first call over a Rocky Cab radio I felt like I was broadcasting live from WOR in New York City. I was a nervous wreck. I was sent to a grocery store for a three-dollar fare. No tip. First blood.

"Listen up, Tenderfoot," Big Al said. He has referred to me as "Tenderfoot" ever since my first day on the job. I like to think it's a term of endearment but it's probably just an insult. "Aside from the fact that the rumor mill said you killed that girl, I don't know anything about her, and I don't want to know. But when a cab driver makes the tactical error of giving bad advice to a fare, it reflects on all of us drivers. If this wannabe starlet goes down in flames, or even worse, gets a role in a sitcom, you will never be able to show your face again at DIA. You'll be branded."

"This isn't about me," I said, getting a bit miffed.

"Yes it is," he said. "It's about your redemption."

That's the way he phrased it. But I knew what he was really saying, i.e., "You're making her pay for your mistake, Tenderfoot, and you have to set things right. It's time to gird your loins and become a true asphalt warrior. Go now—and bring her back alive."

I pocketed the money and stood up. "Thanks, Big Al. I don't know how I can pay you back."

"For starters, you can pay me back the fifty bucks I gambled on you," he said.

I pulled the money out and peeled off a fifty. "What about paying back the rest of this dough?" I said.

"It isn't real," he said. "It's found money. But when you do bring this girl home, as I know you will, put her in first class. You fly coach. That's an order. And while you're chewing on those rock-hard peanuts and sipping a warm soda, I want you to think about your sins."

"All of them?" I said.

"As many as you can cram into a three-hour flight."

CHAPTER 21

Melanie answered the door, and this time I asked if I could come inside and talk with her. She was hesitant. I knew the feeling. I was like a "pedestrian," a fare who opens the door to my cab without warning, someone who hasn't come out of a hotel or the terminal at DIA, someone who didn't call Rocky Cab for taxi service.

"I'm going to Los Angeles to see if I can bring Alicia back home," I said to her.

She let me in. The apartment was small. It was plastered with movie posters. The walls anyway. I took a quick glance at the bookshelf as I sat down in the living room. Not too many books, and no novels. The books were nonfiction. They were about show business. Nonfiction books about show business? Who's kidding who?

"I'm leaving this afternoon," I said. "Have you heard from Alicia?"

"She said she would call me after she got there," Melanie said. "But she hasn't called yet."

"Does Alicia have any connections in Hollywood?"

"A friend of ours from high school is going to UCLA out there," Melanie said. "Her name is Brenda. She was in *Carousel* with Alicia. Alicia said she was going to look her up."

"Is Brenda a theater major?" I said.

"No, she's an English major."

Fer the luvva Christ. "I suppose she plans to be an English teacher." Melanie shrugged.

I asked for Brenda's address. Melanie was hesitant to give it to me.

"Maybe you would rather give her address to the police," I said. This worked. Brenda gave me the address. She seemed to be really scared of the police. I pegged her as normal.

"When I get out to LA," I said, "I'm going to call you to see if Alicia checked in."

I liked saying "LA." It made me feel important. It made me feel like I didn't have time to say "Los Angeles" because I was too busy cutting deals.

After I got all the information out of Melanie that I needed, I hopped into my heap and headed home. I had a bag to pack. I made quick work of my suitcase. I had learned in my youth to travel light, especially in the army where I found that all you needed was money and your orders— and I had my orders: fly coach.

Okay. I'll admit it. I grabbed a couple of screenplays from my steamer trunk and tossed them into my suitcase.

As I headed for the door I looked at the telephone. There were a couple of calls I could have made. One was to Toby Brown. The other was to Randolph Hightower. I could have called my Maw, too, since the rates were cheaper on weekends, but I didn't make any of those calls, especially to Maw. There was nothing to stop her from hopping a flight here just to grab my ear and drag me to a confessional. There's plenty of Catholic churches in this burg. Instead I called Yellow Cab.

I turned away and walked out the door.

I didn't have long to wait. I tossed my suitcase in the trunk and got in the backseat. When we got to DIA, I could see the staging area where half the city's taxi force was patiently waiting their turn to grab a fifty dollar trip to downtown. I turned away from the window. When I got inside the terminal I tried three different airlines, and grabbed the first flight to LA. One-way. I decided that if I couldn't talk Alicia into coming back with me, maybe I would just stay there. I had nothing waiting for me in Denver, except a surly movie director, an enraged father, and Big Al. Let me try that again. I decided I better never come back at all.

The sky was clear over LA, but the smog wasn't. As the plane began its descent I peered out my window at "The Streets of La-La Land." That was the title of the second screenplay I ever wrote. It was about a kid who moves to LA and tries to write a screenplay about a kid who moves to LA and tries to write a screenplay. My inspiration was Franz Kafka. I quickly learned that nobody in LA had ever heard of Franz Kafka except Orson Welles, and he was in Europe.

After the pilot threw us off the plane, I walked into the terminal and saw a lot of chauffeurs standing around in the waiting area holding cardboard signs with names hand-printed on them. I didn't see my name. It made me feel unimportant.

I walked out of the terminal and looked at a long line of Yellow Cabs waiting for fares. I had the urge to go up to the cabbies and introduce myself and tell them I drove a cab in Denver, but I was afraid they would think I was a rube. Instead I took a shuttle bus to a rental agency and leased a car. I was forced to use my credit card.

You heard me right. I have a credit card. But I almost never use it. In my hands a credit card can be a walking time-bomb. I had learned my lesson when I worked for Dyna-Plex, back when I adhered to the strict rules of American capitalism and lived beyond my means.

After the clerk gave me the keys and a funny look, probably because I was wearing my "big" coat, I stepped outside the agency and took a deep breath. I exhaled with a sigh. It smelled good to be back in LA.

The air was warm. The smog wasn't as dry as it is in Denver, and it contained the distinct undertaste of oranges. There was a fruit stand next to the rental agency. I walked over to my car, a little two-door sedan. I knew my way around town, and knew where I was headed. There was a small motel off Sunset, just west of Hollywood, called the Piedmont. I had stayed there for a week when I first arrived almost twenty years earlier. The rates had been fifty dollars a day back then. I had asked if there were weekly rates and the proprietor said no. I assumed they didn't want anybody living there permanently. The place had silverfish, but the price was right, and this time I didn't plan on staying more than two days. I figured that if it took me more than two days to fail, I should find something harder to do.

I pulled away from LAX and took the 405 up to Santa Monica Boulevard, then headed toward the Hollywood District. I felt like I was coming home. That was how I had felt years ago when I first arrived in LA and began walking the streets gazing at all the glitz. Even then I knew I was in the land of fakes and frauds and phonies—I felt like saying "Howdy cousin," to everybody who walked by.

I found the motel. It looked the same as it had years earlier: shabby. This was something that had surprised me when I first came to LA. I expected Los Angeles to be slick and modern, but overall it had a rundown look and feel to it. Sort of like Denver. Sort of like every city in America I've lived in, except San Francisco, which looks cool.

I entered the manager's office expecting to see the same clerk who had run the joint before, an elderly man who never looked me in the eye from the moment I checked in until the moment I fled the silverfish. I was also expecting to see the same rates, but the price had gone up to seventy-five dollars a day. The clerk was different, too, a young man with a goatee and an earring, both on his chin. I rented a room for the night. After I got inside my room, I checked the shower. The silverfish looked the same.

I tossed my suitcase onto the bed, then made a long-distance call to Melanie in Denver. It was six o'clock in LA, which made it seven in Denver. Melanie was home. She had been waiting for my call.

"Has Alicia gotten in touch with you?" I said.

"Yes."

"Where is she?"

"She's staying at Brenda's. But she told me that she and Brenda are going to a party tonight."

My heart sank. Already Alicia was being sucked into the sewer of show-biz.

"What kind of party?" I said.

"Brenda is going to introduce Alicia to some friends from school."

My heart sank even further. Alicia was being sucked into the sewer of college.

"You didn't tell her I was coming, did you?"

"No, Murph. She doesn't know."

"I appreciate that, Melanie. I'm going to get in touch with her as soon as I can. You haven't heard from Toby or from Alicia's father have you?"

"No."

"Let's keep it that way."

"What should I say if they call me?" she said. She sounded worried. She sounded like an ordinary Jane caught up in a game that had rules she didn't understand.

"Don't volunteer anything," I said. "But whatever they ask, tell them the truth, even if they ask about me."

"All right, I'll do that."

We rang off. I didn't expect Toby to call Melanie, but you never can tell about fathers. Randolph Hightower was the first father of a teenage girl that I had ever gotten along well with, but that's probably because I wasn't dating Alicia.

When I was a teenager, most fathers tended to go berserk when I asked their daughters on a date. After comparing notes with my buddies I discovered that all fathers go berserk when their daughters start dating. I had to assume this was because all fathers were once teenagers at some point in their lives, so they had no illusions about whether or not the boys were "up to something." But what really baffled me was the fact that the mothers never seemed to get upset, even though they must have known that the boys were "up to something." The existence of their daughters was proof of that. I sometimes think all mothers are "up to something" and I'm not sure I want to know what it is.

I took a quick shower, said howdy to the silverfish, then dried and got dressed. I had somewhere to go. It was an address on Stanley Avenue.

It was getting dark out. At a quarter to seven I found the apartment building where Brenda lived. I parked on the street, walked up to the front door, and peered through the glass. There was a small foyer with a row of buttons on the wall. Same buttons you see in every foyer in America. I bet the guy who invented doorbells made out okay.

I entered the foyer and found Brenda's apartment number. I pressed the button and waited. Nothing. I expected that. I could have called ahead like a polite person, but I was afraid it would scare Alicia off. I didn't want her to know that I was in town until the moment she saw me. But at least I knew where she was staying. I could check again the next day.

I walked back to my car and was just opening the door when I heard a mechanical grinding sound. I looked around and saw the security door of the underground parking garage opening. A red sports car darted out from the darkness of the garage, then slowed before pulling onto the road. Seated shotgun was the familiar head of a girl who once held a resemblance to Zelda Fitzgerald. She was grinning and chatting with the driver, who must have been Brenda. They looked like what they were— two nubile blondes headed for a party. I had seen plenty of their kind in my life. I watch a lot of TV.

I hopped into my rented heap and took off after them. I had no intention of trying to intercept the sports car, but I wanted to see where it was going. And more than that, I wanted to make sure that both occupants came back when the party was over.

I followed them to Highland Avenue. They turned left and headed north to the 101 and started climbing up the Santa Monica Mountains, the speed bump between LA and the San Fernando Valley.

Okay. I'll admit it. I'm from Colorado so I make fun of other people's mountains.

I then realized that the party wasn't being held within the city limits of Los Angeles proper. My worst fears were coming true. Unless I was mistaken, Brenda's friends lived in The Valley, fer the luvva Christ!

I stomped on the gas and rocketed up the hill toward Cahuenga Pass, my imagination running amok.

CHAPTER 22

One thing you should never do in Los Angeles is speed in the presence of cops.

I realized this when I topped Cahuenga Pass and saw the flashing red lights of a police car up ahead that had pulled someone over near the exit that led into Universal City Studios. I took my foot off the accelerator and rolled past the cruiser, and noticed that the little red sports car in the distance had done the same thing. Smart girl, that Brenda. She was an English major but she knew how to beat John Law at his own game. I always say, if you can't do the time, drive safely.

I stayed with the sports car. We held to the speed limit, cool as cucumbers. As I passed the entrance to Universal City, I remembered the time I visited the place eighteen years earlier. I'll admit it. I took the tour. I rode the tram. I snapped a picture of the *Psycho* house. I even saw the *Jaws* shark as it made a pass at us near a low bridge. But I was sitting on the wrong side of the tram so I didn't get a good photo. It really made me mad.

Then we were in The Valley. I didn't know The Valley very well. I hadn't gone there much when I was delivering ice cream and trying to finish my first screenplay. I didn't own a car in those days. I lived within walking distance of the ice cream distribution warehouse, which made it difficult to lie and call in sick. One time I called in a lie, and they sent a kid named Brad over to check up on me because they actually believed I was sick and wanted to help me. I'll never understand California.

The sports car got onto the Ventura Freeway and headed toward Sherman Oaks. It exited at Van Nuys Boulevard and cut south. The car began a short climb through a series of winding streets in the "foothills" of the "mountains." I tried not to make it obvious that I was following the sports car. This consisted of pulling over and stopping every now and then, shutting off my lights, then turning them on and going forward again. I figured this would be an excellent method of shadowing someone. I'll admit it. I'm not the world's greatest shadower, but I've done it a few times. It works best in a cab. Cabs make good camouflage. I once shadowed a guy who came out of a K-Mart. He walked toward his car in the parking lot and I followed him at a discreet distance. I wanted his parking space. He put some packages into his trunk and went back to the K-Mart. It really made me mad.

Then the sports car pulled up in front of a house. There were five other automobiles parked out front. No sidewalks on the hill. It was an asphalt street, dirt shouldered, and heavy with shade trees. Brenda parked behind a sports car. All the cars were sports. California is a swinging state. Lights were on in the house. It was a fancy house. Not as fancy as Randolph Hightower's but I bet it cost as much. California is an expensive state. That's why I live in Denver. Colorado is a cheap state. You see a lot of California license plates in Colorado nowadays. The Word is out.

I pulled to the side of the road and watched as Brenda and Alicia climbed out and followed a flagstone sidewalk up to the front door. I drove forward and slowed next to Brenda's car. I watched as the front door opened. The two young women were greeted by an elderly man with a trim beard. He had a pipe in his mouth. The kind of pipe you smoke. He held the door wide and escorted them inside. My blood began to boil. I pegged him as an English professor. His jacket had patches on the elbows.

The door closed. I heard music wafting from a window. It wasn't rock 'n' roll. It sounded like a chorus from the opera *Carmen*. That was another strike against Professor Patches. I felt like running up the sidewalk and kicking down the door and demanding to see his graduate thesis. I stayed cool though. I wondered what the hell Alicia was doing hanging out with intellectuals when she was supposed to be schmoozing with phonies.

Maybe I was wrong though. Maybe Patches wasn't an English professor at all. There are a lot of phonies in southern California. Maybe he was a talent agent passing himself off as a book lover. Strike three, pal.

I tried to remain calm. I unclenched my teeth. My imagination was running amok again. Twice in one night. This never happens when I'm sitting in front of a typewriter. I'm lucky if my imagination runs amok once a month in Denver. But maybe it had something to do with the fact that I was in LA, the show-biz capital of the world. Just being there made me feel creative. I get the same feeling reading fan magazines. Don't even get me started on Oscar night.

That was the beginning of a long sentinel. I got hungry. I cruised down the hill and found a drive-in and ate a burger with fries. I remembered a scene from *Double Indemnity* where Fred MacMurray stopped at a drive-in. The carhop put a bottle of beer on the tray hooked to his door. That made me laugh and laugh. What the hell kind of crazy state lets people drink beer in their cars? But maybe Billy Wilder made that part up. I didn't know, and I didn't want to know. It was like analyzing a Shakespearean sonnet—you destroy something when you parse a poem. I didn't want to destroy the poetry of beer drinking.

I circled past the party house every now and then, keeping an eye on the sports cars. I grew concerned that the neighbors might note that the same car kept rolling by every so often. But I didn't see any neighbors looking out their doors or windows. Maybe people who lived in ritzy houses didn't worry about surreptitious automobiles. Maybe the ritzy houses were filled with fat cats who never worried about anything. Money does that to people, lulls them into a false sense of security. Or maybe it lulls them into an authentic sense of security. That's plausible. If I ever win the lottery, I'll let you know which way I'm lulled.

Then the front door opened. I had already driven past the house twenty times. I felt like a lovesick teenager shadowing a girl he was afraid to ask on a date. Her name was Vicki Demarko, but let's move on. I slowed and looked back to get a gander. It was just a boy and a girl leaving the party. I started to toe the gas when suddenly I recognized the girl. It was Alicia. I didn't recognize the boy, but I was positive he wasn't Brenda.

I pulled my foot away from the accelerator and looked in my rear-view mirror. The couple approached a blue sports car. The boy opened the passenger door and Alicia hopped in, then Sir Galahad walked around the front and got in the driver's side. I pulled over to the shoulder and turned off my lights. I watched as the headlights on the blue car flashed on and the car pulled away. Except for my eyeballs, I sat perfectly still as the car came toward me. I got a good look at Alicia as she passed within four feet of me. She was talking, waving one hand, and wiggling her fingers. I got the impression she was describing something. If not, don't ask me what the hell she was doing.

I wanted to go back to the house and pound on the door and ask Professor Pipesucker who the hell that punk was with Alicia, but it was too late. I yanked on my headlights, pulled away from the shoulder and started following Kid Galahad. I was seething inside, but my seethe was directed at myself as much as at that sun-bleached beach boy who was doubtless "up to something." Big Al was right. I was entirely to blame for this mess. Not one day in the big city and already Alicia had been picked up at a party by some cocky undergrad—he looked like a USC type, the bastard.

Pretty soon we were on Ventura Boulevard headed toward the 101. I gave up all pretense at shadowing. I stayed right on his tail. He didn't seem to notice. I was driving pretty much the way everyone drives in LA, like elephants dancing on each other's backs at a circus. If Hogan had seen me he would have torn up my Herdic. I wouldn't have blamed him—by the time we got over Cahuenga Pass and down into LA, I had committed at least three of the basic rules for unsafe driving: speeding, following too close, and stupidity. I've been told by Denver cops that "stupidity" is the primary cause of traffic accidents. But I felt reckless. I felt like a naked madman running through a bowling alley. I'm not kidding, that's exactly how I felt. There are some things about me I don't want to know.

I wasn't sure what I was going to do when the blue sports car stopped and Act Two of the intellectual stud's filthy scenario came into play. I was winging it. Imagine my surprise when the car pulled up in front of Brenda's apartment building and Alicia got out. I pulled up behind the car and stopped. I heard Alicia call out, "Thanks, Albert!" as she shut the door.

Albert. What the hell kind of name was that for a degenerate? I watched as Sir Albert waited while Alicia walked up to the apartment building and entered the foyer. She worked the door with a key, opened it, then turned and gave her chauffeur a little wave before closing the door behind her.

The blue sports car pulled away from the curb. I watched its taillights disappear in the direction of Sunset Boulevard. I looked at the apartment building. As far as I could figure, Alicia and Brenda had gone to a party, and Brenda had wanted to stay late, so Alicia had solicited a ride from a student of English literature. He had driven her home, waited outside until she was safely inside her building, then drove off. I examined this theory from every angle, and came to the conclusion that I was a moron. I have an instinct for these things.

Did I actually believe Alicia was going to fly out to Los Angeles and immediately become embroiled in a swinging scene involving a sleazy producer and end up drug addicted, pregnant, brokenhearted, and washed up before Day Two?

You be the judge.

I sat outside the building for a few minutes and thought about going up to the foyer and ringing her bell. It was only a little after ten. But somehow I didn't think a young woman would be thrilled if I showed up at her door in the dark unannounced. I've been there and it can get ugly. I decided to stick with my original unsold script and come back in the morning and talk to Alicia after she had a good night's sleep. Of course I did understand that it was probably exciting for Alicia to come to LA and go to a party right off the bat, and I couldn't blame her for doing it. And so what if it involved English majors? There are worse things in this world.

I put the rental into gear and pulled away from the curb. I drove back toward my motel. I was tired and edgy. I stopped at a 7-11 on the way and bought a Twinkie. I ate it as I drove. It calmed me down. It made me feel like I was back in 127 pulling a night shift on the mean streets of Denver, looking for the zombies, the night crawlers, the people who "do things" after the sun goes down. Think of what it must have been like back in the olden days before the lightbulb was invented. I bet hardly anybody did anything after the sun went down. I sometimes think Tom Edison caused more trouble than he was worth.

When I got back to my motel room, I looked at the phone and wondered if I was making a mistake in not calling Randolph Hightower. Thanks to me, his daughter had run off to Hollywood and Randolph didn't even know about it. He had gotten upset enough when she was living at a two-bit amateur film ranch, so I wanted to fix things before he found out where she was now. This is how I always work. Whenever I manage to screw things up royally, I immediately try to fix them before anyone finds out. I did it when I was a kid in Blessed Virgin Grade School in Wichita, and I did it in the army, and I have to say that it generally worked out—but maybe only because I had done it so often that I had gotten good at it. I couldn't begin to tell you the number of times in my youth that I had successfully avoided getting caught, blamed, punished, or even chased. The Boy Scout motto is "Be Prepared," and I interpreted that to mean be prepared to fix the things I wrecked. It's ironic that they don't award merit badges for that proficiency, given the fact that it's the #1 survival skill on earth.

I looked around the motel room for a TV remote but couldn't find one. Then I realized the management wouldn't have provided one anyway—I had already put three of those tiny soaps into my suitcase. I walked across the room and reached up to turn on the TV manually. The prospect of changing the channel manually all evening was ultimately too overwhelming for me to handle. It made me feel like an amputee—a third arm seemed to be missing. I didn't dare look in a newspaper to see how many episodes of *Gilligan* were currently running. I just didn't want to know, that's all there was to it.

I finally worked up the courage to hit the off switch, then I crashed for the night. I hadn't really expected to accomplish anything on my first day in Los Angeles, and so far I was batting a thousand.

CHAPTER 23

I was out the door at eight the next morning. I made a quick stop at McDonald's for an egg McMuffin and a cup of West-Coast joe, then I headed for Alicia's apartment building. I wanted to get this over with quickly. Believe it or not, I have never been a big fan of putting things off, in the sense that if it's not going to work, let's make it not work as soon as possible.

I had considered calling ahead to let Alicia know I was coming, but I had seen enough TV shows to believe that she might disappear on me. I wouldn't be where I am today if it wasn't for TV.

I pulled up in front of her building. On the seat next to me was a paper sack containing a McMuffin and two sausage sandwiches. I didn't bring any coffee for her. I didn't want to be holding a boiling hot cup in my hand when she slammed the door in my face. I've been there.

I climbed out with the sack and walked up the sidewalk, entered the foyer, and pushed the button for Brenda's apartment. I waited. It was a long wait. Then a voice came over the loudspeaker. "Who is it?"

I recognized the voice. It was Alicia. She sounded sleepy. I wished I had brought some joe.

"It's Murph," I said.

"Murph who?" she said with a yawn—a standard female response.

"Murph the taxi driver," I said. "I came here from Denver to talk to you."

No response. I waited.

"What do you want?" she finally said.

"I want to talk to you before the police get here."

I had another long wait. Long enough for a girl to get dressed and hurry down to a foyer and yank open a door. Evidence indicates that's what happened. Alicia looked at me, her eyes filled with both surprise and fear, another standard female response to my sudden appearances. I quickly held up the sack. "I brought you breakfast. It's piping hot."

The surprise melted away, but the fear stayed. She looked at the sack, then looked at me. "How did you find me?" she said.

"That's not important," I said, "What's important is that you eat this before it gets cold."

She looked confused. She looked off balance. That's a technique I employ to get dates, and it always works. She closed her eyes and sighed. "Come in," she said.

It was a small place. Kitchenette/dining room, with a bedroom off to the side. It was like a dorm room. Made sense. Brenda was an English major. I set the sack on the kitchen table but Alicia didn't look at it. "What's this about the police?" she said.

"You took the demo reel without permission," I said. "The police might have to get involved."

"I did so have permission," she said. This brought me up short.

"From who?"

"From Toby."

"He told me he didn't know anything about it," I said.

She shrugged and sat down at the table, opened the sack, and peeked into it.

"Are you saying Toby lied to me?" I said.

She shrugged again. She acted like she wasn't worried. All of a sudden I was worried enough for both of us. I reached out and lifted the sack off the table. She pouted. It wasn't an act. She was really pouting. I know my pouts.

"Why would Toby lie to me about that?" I said.

"Toby told me that when the demo reel was finished I could show it to people," she said. "He said I could use it to get a job in the movies."

"So?"

"He said we were finished shooting, so I took the reel and came out here."

"Without telling him you were coming here?"

She nodded. "It wasn't any of his business. He said I could have the reel."

It was at this point that I realized I was talking to an eighteen-year-old girl. I placed the sack on the table and sat down on a chair opposite. "What do you plan on doing with the reel?" I said.

"Show it to a producer."

"What producer?"

She shrugged. "There's lots of producers in this town."

"How do you plan on meeting producers?" I said.

"At parties," she said.

"Like the party you went to last night?"

Her eyes widened. "How did you know I went to a party last night?"

"Melanie told me. I talked to her on the phone. I called her last night. I'm staying at the Piedmont over near Sunset Boulevard."

She held my eyes for a moment, then looked down at the table.

"Oh," she said.

"Melanie is the one who told me you came out here. She said you asked her not to tell anyone where she was going. But I made her tell me. I told her you might be in trouble with the police for taking that reel. She said you were going to a party last night. She was trying to help you."

Alicia glanced at me, then looked back at the table.

"Just like I'm doing," I said.

She looked up at me with her lips pursed. "You're starting to sound like my father."

"Good," I said.

"My father doesn't want me to be an actress."

"What makes you think you can act?" I said.

She glared at me. "The demo reel," she said. "Toby told me it was great."

"That's his job," I said. "Directors get paid to lie to actresses. It's the producer's job to tell the truth."

"What do you mean?" she said.

"Your father is the executive producer of the demo reel. Your father financed it. That's his demo reel."

"I thought …"

"I know what you thought. It's what we wanted you to think. But you don't have any talent, Alicia. Talent is something you develop, you're not born with it."

"I do so have talent."

"Your father told me that you don't. But he wasn't being mean, he was being honest. All you have right now is good looks and ambition. You and the five thousand other girls who came to LA yesterday from Iowa."

Her face went pale. For a moment I thought she was going to cry. But then her face got hard. "I'm eighteen years old and I can do what I want. Toby said I could have the reel. I don't care who financed it. I'm going to show it to a producer and he's going to give me an acting job."

"What producer?" I said.

"A guy I met."

"At the party?" She nodded.

"Melanie told me you were going to a party to meet some friends from school."

"I did," she said. "But they all weren't school kids. There were other people there."

"Like producers?"

"Yes."

I wanted to ask her about Mister Blue Sports Car, but I couldn't. I didn't want her to know I had shadowed her.

I sat back in the chair and nodded. "You're right," I said. "You're eighteen, and old enough to do what you want. And you're smart. You've been here barely a day and you've already made contacts. You're on your way. But what are you going to do when the producer watches your demo reel and finds out you can't act?"

"I can so act!" she said. She was livid. "I had the lead role in *Carousel* when I was in high school!"

"So did your mother," I said. "And where's her film career?"

Alicia gave me an eye roll. "My mother never tried to be a film star."

Suddenly I knew. I got a cold chill up my spine. I wanted to tell Alicia what I knew, but it stuck in my throat. So instead I said, "How do you know your mother never tried to be a film star?"

Alicia gave me a hard look.

I took a deep breath and sighed. "Listen, Alicia. It's a good thing for you to have ambition and want to become an actress, but you can't just do it. It doesn't just happen because you want it to happen. You've got to know how to do it. You've got to take acting lessons and get roles in plays and develop your skills. I knew plenty of actresses when I was in college and I know what it takes. It takes time and study and work. You don't just run out to Hollywood and get a job as an actress."

"Albert said it's possible."

I swallowed hard. "Who's Albert?"

"He's the producer I met at the party last night. He's going to look at my demo reel today."

I knew it now—"Albert" was the perfect name for a degenerate.

"So if that's all you wanted to say to me, then you probably should leave now," Alicia said. "I've got an appointment to meet Albert for lunch. We're going to Spago. Then he's going to look at the demo reel in the screening room at his office."

"Where's his office?"

"In Century City."

I hadn't noticed, but Alicia had eaten the McMuffin and both sausage sandwiches. She wadded up the papers and stuffed them into the sack.

"Thank you for coming out here, Murph. And thank you for breakfast. But you can tell my father that I'm not coming back to Denver."

"He doesn't know you're here," I said.

She stared at me for a moment, then said, "I don't believe you."

I stood up from the table and looked down at her. "Believe me," I said. "I came out here on my own. Your father didn't have anything to do with it. He doesn't know I'm here. I was hoping I could talk you out of this idea that you're going to become a movie star. I've been around creative people all my life. Most of the cab drivers I know are trying to become novelists. I'm a failed novelist myself. But you're right. You're legally old enough to make your own decisions. Legally old enough to break your parents' hearts."

I picked up the paper sack, carried it to a wastebasket, and dropped it in. "I'm going now," I said. "Good luck with your acting career."

I headed for the door.

"Wait a minute, Murph."

I turned. Alicia was squinting at me. "Why did you do this? Why did you come out here?"

"Guilt," I said. "If it wasn't for me, you wouldn't be sitting at this table. If it wasn't for me, that demo reel would never have gotten made. You'd still be in Denver making short subjects with Toby and dreaming about going to Hollywood. If it wasn't for me ..." I almost said you wouldn't turn out just like your mother.

Instead I walked out. That was that. I had ruined another human being's life and I wasn't able to fix it. I had been a lousy Boy Scout. I was never prepared for anything. I never made it past Tenderfoot.

I climbed into my heap and headed west. I didn't want to go back to my motel. I didn't want to go back to Denver. I had blown it. Who was I to think I could save a girl from trying to do what millions of girls had tried to do ever since George Eastman figured out how to glue light-sensitive chemicals to celluloid? Jaysus, how in the hell did he do that?

I kept driving west. I thought about driving past the apartment building where I had lived almost two decades ago, delivering ice cream, pounding out my first screenplay, and thinking about the ways I was going to spend my first million. My big dream back then was to buy an IBM Selectric. I still have that dream. I really ought to buy a word-processor. Half the cabbies at Rocky own computers. They tell me they can write failed novels ten times faster on a PC.

I kept driving west. One of the handy things about Los Angeles is that you can't drive west very long. Pretty soon you hit the Pacific Ocean if you don't stop. I didn't feel like stopping. I felt like driving right off the Santa Monica pier. How could I go back to Denver and face Big Al? How could I spend the rest of my life branded?

Pretty soon I was at the western edge of Santa Monica, eyeing the end of the long pier. A lot of people were fishing off the pier. Fishing is one sport I understand. You just sit. Some people stand. I don't understand some people. I used to spend a lot of time at the beach in Santa Monica. I would go there on my days off and search for inspiration. Then I would go back to my pad and write a scene about a kid wandering the beach in search of inspiration. It didn't work. There was something missing from my screenplay. It was the same thing missing from my life: a plot.

I decided to park the rental and head down to the beach and take a look around. Old home week if you get my drift. I wondered if much had changed. It hadn't. Same tourists lying on the beach. Same gray sand. Same crappy stucco buildings. I loved it. I felt young again. It wasn't a good feeling. Can you love something and hate it at the same time? Yes. I saw young guys wandering around who looked like I did when I came out to LA looking for The Big Break. Guys who would be heading back to their pads to work on their own unsold screenplays. I tried not to think about it.

I looked for the guy who juggled chainsaws. He wasn't there. I watched the weightlifters. I thought about Steve Reeves. *Hercules* was my favorite movie when I was ten years old. *Hercules Unchained* was my second favorite movie. According to Leonard Maltin, both movies were filmed in Dyaliscope.

I wandered the sidewalk watching all the street performers doing their juggling acts, playing their musical instruments, busting their asses to avoid work. I liked that. But I wanted to tell them there were easier ways to avoid work, like cab driving. I was through giving advice though. I vowed that as long as I drove I would never again give any advice. If a fare ever asked me for advice, I would tell him I was from Czechoslovakia.

And then, as I was walking past a crappy little stucco storefront, I noticed a sign that said, "The Cult Hut."

CHAPTER 24

I stepped inside. I was immediately struck by an odor which reminded me of marijuana, but that didn't mean a thing. The building obviously had been there for decades, back through the swinging '60s and beat '50s and hipster '40s, and surely had soaked up the atmosphere of all that West Coast ambience—although the proprietor could have been toking a bong in the back room. The point being that it had a musty odor of the type you might associate with a quaint bookshop except the must was leafy rather than fungoid. I dug it. I began thinking in groovy lingo.

The Cult Hut turned out to be a video store. Rent or buy. There were narrow aisles packed with video boxes reaching to the ceiling. It was cloying. I edged my way into the store gazing at the titles, which explained the name of the store. It specialized in cult videos. I recognized a lot of the stuff going back through Russ Meyer and Herschel Gordon Lewis, and of course Roger Corman, the kinds of movies that came out when I was a kid and were condemned not only by the Catholic Church, but by The-Last-Word-On-The-Subject—my Maw. There was also a lot of stuff that I had managed to see, from science fiction like *Plan 9 From Outer Space* to later stuff where the Baby Boomers tried to cash in on the cult craze by making ersatz cult movies, which of course were an insult to anyone with a predilection toward originality in depravity. Which is to say, Ed Wood was doing the best he could with what he had, which wasn't much. But to deliberately make a bad movie ... well ... the English professors have a word for it: "going commercial." Okay—two words, prof.

The proprietor was seated on a stool by the cash register, which was located in another room accessed by a Dutch door. A square hole had been cut into the storefront adjacent to allow for expansion of The Cult Hut. The proprietor was like Rollo in his cage. He had a beret tugged low on his scalp. His cheeks and chin were like Popeye's, though tanned, but not healthy surfer tanned—more like he'd lived in California all his life and couldn't escape tanned. He was wearing a moss-green turtleneck pullover. I think he was older than me. He was smoking the stub of a cigarette. Cigarettes make people look older. That's why I took up smoking when I was sixteen. I wanted to look older. I also wanted people to think I was cool. The tobacco companies probably thought I was cool. They got ten grand out of me before I quit.

"What's popping?" I said, trying to sound cool.

The proprietor gave me a brief smile, a squint-eyed nod. He was cooler than me and I knew it. I gave up trying.

"Do you have a movie called *The Man Who Crawled Across Denver?*" I said. I knew he wouldn't have it. I was just trying to make friendly conversation. But the guy perked up.

"Naw," he said, his voice hoarse. "Who directed it?"

"Antoine Baroni," I said.

He began tapping the tips of his teeth together. He looked down at the countertop. He was thinking. I've seen plenty of people do that. He looked up at me. "I never heard of him."

"He's a director in Denver, Colorado."

"Oh yeah, Colorado, Stan Brakhage," he said. "We got some Brakhage if you're looking for Brakhage."

"No, I'm just browsing. This is a great place."

He nodded. He knew it. He didn't need anybody to tell him. There was nothing like this place in Denver. I realized right at that moment that Denver would always be Denver. I didn't want to go back to Denver. I wanted to rent a corner of The Cult Hut and live there for the rest of my life.

I decided I had to get out of there. The place was breaking my heart. It was like watching *Goldfinger* and seeing all those yellow bricks in Fort Knox that I would never get my hands on. I smiled at the guy and nodded preparatory to saying goodbye without giving him any money, when suddenly it popped out of my mouth. "Do you carry a tape called *Summer Kicks*?"

He raised his chin and tilted his eyes away from the smoke as he looked at me. "*Summer Kicks*," he whispered around the stub. "I think I do have that."

"You do?" I said, sounding like the rube that I was.

"I think so," the guy said, and he came off his stool like some kind of legless slime creature, just sort of rolled off it and opened the Dutch door and glided into the main room and disappeared down a narrow aisle. He was like a goddamn troll. I followed him. I peeked around a corner and saw his fingers like big brown spiders running up a wall of tapes. He plucked a tape and held it close to his eyes, then glided toward me, whisked past me, and went back to his lair. He rolled up onto his stool and set the tape in front of him, picked up a feather duster from below the counter and began brushing the cardboard box. He held it up so I could see the artwork. My jaw dropped two inches. Literally. It was Mrs. Hightower in a bikini. And she wasn't just an extra: Starring Beverly Burke.

I won't describe what Mrs. Hightower looked like in a bikini when she was eighteen. This ain't France.

"Does it get rented very often?" I said.

"I been working here nine years and I never rented it yet," he said, giving the box a few theatrical brushes with his fingertips. A last residue of dust drifted to the desktop.

"Have you ever seen it?" I said.

"When I was a teenager," he said.

"Any good?"

"Piece of garbage."

"How much to rent it?"

"Two bucks a night."

"Know where I can rent a video player?" I said. "I'm in town for a couple days and I'm staying at a motel."

"Do you have a credit card?" he said. He destroyed something when he said that. The romance of the troll. It's all about money in the end, but I always knew that. Even James Joyce complained when the retail sales of *Finnegans Wake* fell short of his ludicrous expectations.

That night I sat alone in my motel room and watched *Summer Kicks* on a VCR rented from The Cult Hut.

How early is too early in Hollywood? I've read stories about people who get up before dawn and head for a studio and work all day and don't get back until after dark, then hit the sack as soon as they get home. I've read stories about people who party all night, hit the sack at dawn, and don't get up until late afternoon. That describes my college career. But how do you know when it's too early to phone someone in the show-biz capital of the world? I had to wing it. I had to pretend I was not in a city with a checkerboard time zone. I had this idea that I should call Alicia around ten in the morning. But I was afraid it might be too late, that she might already be in makeup in some fly-by-night production company. They say Hollywood is driven by fear, and I was getting a taste of it.

I ultimately did the only thing I knew how to do, but knew how to do well. Since I was dealing with an industry grounded in pretending, I pretended I was in the real world and that ten A.M. was a perfectly reasonable hour to call someone. It worked. I don't know why I waste so much energy on self-doubt.

"Hello?"

"Alicia?"

"Yes."

"This is Murph."

Silence.

I gritted my teeth. I had spent a lot of time during my youth talking into the silence of women, and I'd never gotten used to it.

"What do you want?" she finally said. A standard female response.

"I just wanted to let you know that I'm leaving Los Angeles and going back to Denver."

"Oh!" she responded perkily.

"So I just wanted to call and wish you luck. I'm sure that you didn't especially appreciate me trying to talk you out of your plans. After all, what you do with your life is entirely your business. I just hope you understand that I did it because I was concerned about you, what with my having set up your demo reel and arranging the funding and all that. I was just trying to help you. Trying to help people is one of my character flaws."

There was a lilt of laughter in her voice when she said, "Well thank you, Murph," but I couldn't tell whether she got the joke or was just happy that I was leaving town. Perhaps a bit of both.

"There is one thing though, Alicia."

Silence again. It's odd how you can sense human vibes through copper wire. Alexander Graham Bell was a genius.

"What is it?" she said.

"It's just this, Alicia. I told you that I'm a failed novelist as well as a failed screenwriter. I've written a lot of screenplays during the past twenty years, but I've never gotten a producer to look at anything of mine. So what with me being responsible for setting up the demo reel, and making it possible for you to come out here to Hollywood and develop contacts with people in the industry, I was wondering if you might be willing to do me a small favor?"

"What's that?" she said suspiciously. All women are alike.

"I was wondering if you would be willing to slip one of my screenplays to your friend Albert."

The silence at the other end of the line had the peculiar quality of possessing no vibes at all. I understood why. This was probably the first time Alicia had run into someone like me, a failed screenwriter looking for an "in." She hadn't yet mastered the art of fending off chumps.

"I suppose I could do that for you," she said. "I'm going to see him later today."

"Swell!" I said, feigning excitement. Or was I? "Are you going to meet him in Century City? I could give him my screenplay right there in his office."

"You mean you want to meet him in person?" she said.

"Oh that would even be better, thanks," I said.

I felt so evil that I knew I would be chewing a lot of rock-hard peanuts on the flight home.

There was a slight rustle at the other end of the line—the sound of someone changing ears. I worked fast.

"I mean it would be great if you could give him my screenplay, but it would be nicer if I could hand it to himself myself so I could pitch my idea to him. I read in a book that pitching stories in person can be an effective way of selling screenplays."

"Well the thing is, Murph, I'm going out to Albert's beach house in Malibu this afternoon." Bell's receiver almost cracked in my fist. "Albert is having a party for some movie people," she continued, "and he wants me to meet them."

My grip relaxed, but my teeth remained clenched. Movie people. I had read all about movie people.

I cleared my throat and swallowed hard. "As a favor to me, could you ask Albert if I could drop by his beach house for a minute, just to give him the screenplay? I don't plan to hang around. I have an eight o'clock flight to Denver so I'll just barely have time to run by and drop it off."

"I suppose I could ask him."

"Just as a favor to me, that's all," I said, pretending to sound logical. She fell for it.

"Can I call you back?" she said.

I gave her my number, then hung up the phone and gritted my teeth. This was a long shot. For all I knew I would never hear from Alicia again. The phone rang. I picked it up. She told me Albert would be delighted to take a peek at my opus.

"Opus means screenplay," she said with a giggle.

"I know what it means," I said.

"Albert is so funny," she said.

She gave me directions to the beach house in Malibu.

I hung up the phone. I had things to do. If I was doomed to be redeemed, I had to work fast. I opened my suitcase and reached in and grabbed at random one of my screenplays, just as I had packed the screenplays at random. I took a quick look at the title in case Albert asked me what it was called. "Beneath the Planet of the Chain-Gang Beach Bunnies." Oh yeah—I remembered this one. It was post-college. I was living in Detroit at the time, working on a loading dock. It was winter. It was cold. It was snowing hard, so I wrote a suspense science fiction adventure that takes place on a warm beach. That and a couple gallons of joe got me through the Detroit freeze. The fact that I had grabbed at random a beach movie made my heart soar. It was kismet. I could feel it.

I gathered up the VCR and tape, and headed out the door. I drove back to the beach at Santa Monica. I had to pick up a few necessities.

I locked all my valuables in the trunk, even the screenplay, then I took a little walk. I dodged the Rollerbladers and panhandlers and finally came to a tented stall that sold shirts, hats, sandals, and sunglasses. I needed shades if I was going to talk to a producer. I didn't want to blow this deal by looking like me.

I found a long table stacked with sunglasses. I tried on a few pairs and studied my mug in a mirror hooked to a tent pole. I wanted to create a certain impression. I didn't want the shades to make me look too cool, yet I didn't want to look like I wasn't hip. And I didn't want them to make me appear pushy, yet I didn't want to look as reclusive as Garbo.

I found a somewhat conservative pair that had just a bit of flair. It's rather difficult to describe the sunglasses, so let's just say I looked somewhere between coolish and hippish, without appearing pushy or reclusive. I was satisfied. Then I went looking for a shirt, the kind of shirt that a screenwriter on-the-make might wear to a beach house. I normally wear T-shirts, but I felt the one I had on might appear a little too informal for a swinging Hollywood bash. It looked sort of "Denver," if you get my drift.

Again, not too cool but not unhip—flair minus the pushy, that was my goal. I noticed that a lot of the dudes Rollerblading at Venice Beach wore colorful shirts, untucked and flairy, yet neither overbearing nor reclusive. I decided to adopt that look. It had been a long time since I had worn a long shirt untucked. I once got fired from a job for refusing to tuck in my shirt, but let's not get into that.

I bought a shirt that had giant pink petunias on it. On the way back to my car I stopped at a booth and bought a plastic cupholder. Souvenir of Venice Beach. I bought it for my '64 Chevy back in Denver. It needed a cupholder bad. Real bad. I carried my gear to my rented car and sat in the driver's seat trying to figure out how to remove the price tag. I didn't have a knife or scissors or anything, so I bit it off, hoping nobody would see me acting uncool. But I didn't care. I would never see any of these panhandlers again, if I was lucky.

I pulled off my T-shirt and put on my flowery shirt, slipped on my sunglasses, and looked at myself in the rear-view mirror. I had to sort of wiggle the mirror up and down to see all of myself. Goddamn but I looked good—a screenwriter on the make, headed for his first pitch.

I backed the rental out of the slot and pointed the hood ornament south toward Malibu. I drove for half a mile, then made a quick U-turn. I remembered that Malibu was north of Venice.

CHAPTER 25

You've seen them in the movies. Wooden houses on stilts. Big windows. Unpainted walls. Broad beachfronts. Is this how the Founding Fathers envisioned our manifest destiny—cracker boxes filled with actors?

I followed a dirt road toward a cluster of rustic structures. There was a kind of informal parking area on the sand with sports cars crowded around. I didn't see any rental cars. When I got closer I saw the blue sports car. There were a lot of red ones, and a single yellow one. Did I mention that my car was gray? It made me feel uncool. But after I parked, I wiggled my rear-view mirror to restore the old confidence. It worked.

I got out and adjusted my shirt and shades, then opened the trunk and grabbed my screenplay and the VHS copy of *Summer Kicks,* which I tucked into my back pocket. I left the parking area and started trudging through the sand, following footprints. Some of them veered off toward the first house, and some continued on to the second house a little farther along. That was Albert's house. There was a third house still farther with a few footprints headed in that direction, but most of the feet turned toward Albert's. That's where the big party was today. I could hear music on a stereo. I could see people standing around on a patio with drinks in their hands. It looked like what it was—a Malibu beach party. That might make a good title for a movie. I'm a chronic extrapolator. I trudged my way toward a set of wooden steps that led up to the patio. The first thing I noticed was that no one on the deck was wearing shades. Totally uncool.

"Is this Albert's place?" I said as I made the top step.

Two women looked over at me and smiled. They nodded. I might as well get this over with. They were babes. All the women at the party were babes. Some of them were wearing bikinis and some were wearing regular clothes. Nuff said. Let's keep moving.

"Is Albert around?" I said.

One of the women was holding a martini glass, her arms akimbo. She sauntered over to me and said, "Albert's inside. Who are you?"

"Murph," I said.

"What do you do?"

"I write screenplays."

She smiled and sauntered back to her friend. I never saw her again.

I stepped up to a big sliding glass door and looked inside. It was a cozy scene. A group of people were crowded around a coffee table, and unless I was mistaken, they were playing Yahtzee. They were hunched over the table. Dice would roll, there would be a burst of laughter, and bodies would peel back like human flower-petals in a Busby Berkeley movie. That's when I saw Alicia. She was sitting next to Blue Sports Car.

"Triples!" Blue Boy exclaimed. I got a good look at him, better than the look I had gotten when he drove Alicia home. He was older than I had thought, hovering around thirty. He was tanned. But who wasn't? Alicia, that's who. She was wearing a light-colored blouse and slacks. She was seated too close to Albert for my comfort. But then everybody was seated close together—Yahtzee does that to people.

Albert raised the canister of dice and rattled it, glancing around the room as he did so. Then he saw me. The can slowed. The rattle faded. He turned to Alicia and said something, and she looked over at me. A smile blossomed on her lips, thank God. That doesn't always happen when women see me, even when they're expecting me. When they're not expecting me, it gets worse.

Alicia stood up and grabbed Albert's hand. He followed her up. He was wearing shorts and a long shirt like mine, except it didn't have the flair mine did.

"Hello Murph!" Alicia said as she approached. She was buzzed and happy. She was eighteen and hanging out with movie people. I expected her to start hopping on her toes any second. "Albert, this is Murph, the screenwriter I told you about."

Albert was a good-looking young guy. I'm always staggered by the existence of successful young people. Where has my life gone?

"Hello Murph," he said, and held out his hand. He looked at me with a completely open-faced and curious expression, his eyebrows raised.

I took it and shook it, but something inside me was wary, like I expected him to judo-toss me into the fireplace. Did I mention that this pad had a fireplace? There was no fire going right then. No. That would come later. I had read stories about producers and their cozy cabanas. I looked at Alicia. She seemed younger than eighteen at that moment. She was filled with joy. It sickened me. But then joy always does that to me. So does optimism and resilience.

"Hello," I said. I took off my sunglasses. This made me feel less cool.

Albert looked me up and down. I had the sense that he was truly curious about me. If Alicia had told him about me, then he probably knew I drove a cab. Probably knew I had helped her with the demo reel. Probably knew things I would never have told him myself. I'm a rather secretive person. It's almost impossible to get me to reveal anything about myself, unless you offer me a drink.

"Would you like a drink?" he said.

"I'm drinking what you're drinking," I said.

"All right," he said. "I'm having cranberry juice."

"Me, too," Alicia said.

Sure, I said to myself. Right now you're giving her cranberry juice, but what about later this evening when the guests are gone and it's time for you and Alicia to get cozy in front of a raging fire and discuss The Deal that's going to turn her into a superstar?

"Okay," I said.

"Come on into the kitchen," Albert said.

The "kitchen" was just a counter on the far side of the room. I had taken in the interior of the house at a glance, and it looked like a two-room bungalow, three if you counted the bathroom. By this I mean a bedroom, a bathroom, and the big room where the party was going on. Fireplace. Television. Bar. Couch. Chairs. Floor. Ceiling. Cozy as hell.

Albert poured me a cran, then poured a couple for himself and Alicia. As he set the bottle down he looked at me and said, "Alicia tells me you drive a taxi."

"That's right," I said.

"A noble calling," he said.

I was so nonplused by this remark that I just stood there staring at him.

"Ted drove a taxi in Seattle before he came down here," he said.

"Who's Ted?" I said.

He pointed toward the Yahtzee table. "That fellow in the blue jeans. He's my line producer."

I looked at Ted. He was younger than me. Everybody in the room was younger than me. I began to experience something like vertigo. I think it was dizziness.

"In fact, Ted drove a taxi here in LA for six months before we got hooked up," Albert said.

I nodded. I didn't know what to say. Was he hinting at something? What was in this cranberry juice? Was I being drugged and set up?

"Is that your screenplay, Murph?" Alicia said.

She sounded like a little girl just trying to be helpful. I glanced at the screenplay clutched in my left hand. Alicia didn't have as much tact as Albert, who had not brought up the only reason I was even at this bash. But I assumed that if Alicia hung out with movie people long enough, she would acquire tact. It could happen to anybody in this crazy town.

"Oh … uh … yes," I said. I lifted it to my chest as if it was a microphone.

Albert folded his arms and smiled at me. "What's your movie about?" he said.

"My movie?"

"Your screenplay."

"Oh. It's … well … it's kind of a … you know … a comic science fiction suspense thing."

He nodded. He didn't bat an eye. He was a pro. "Mind if I take a look at it?" he said.

This struck me as a sort of screwy upside-down tact, since I had come here specifically to give him the screenplay and he knew it.

I handed it to him.

"'Beneath the Planet of the Chain-Gang Beach Bunnies,'" he said, his head bowed as he read the title page.

Alicia gave up a squeal of laughter.

Albert raised his head with a grin stretching his tanned face. "It sounds interesting."

"Oh it is," I said.

This seemed to strike Albert as terribly funny. He laughed aloud and raised an arm and slapped me once on the shoulder. "I'll dive right into this as as soon as I can, Murph," he said. "I should be able to let you know within a day or two what I think of it. Will you be in town long?"

I'll admit it. I started to make up all sorts of lies. Do I have to paint you a picture? For a moment I had forgotten the real reason I had come here, and it didn't have anything to do with a piece-of-garbage screenplay twenty years old.

"No," I said. "I'm leaving tonight. I'm heading back to Denver. I can't stay long."

Albert frowned. It seemed real. When you've driven a taxi as long as I have, you see a lot of frowns in your rear-view mirror. I know my frowns.

"I'm sorry to hear that," Albert said. "Can you stay at the party for a little while? We'd love to have you. I'd like to hear about this friend of yours back in Denver, Toby Brown. Alicia tells me he had a film in the Mile-Hi International Film Festival."

"Yes he did," I said. "It was a short-subject called *The Man Who Crawled Across Denver.*"

"I'd like to have seen it," Albert said. "I couldn't make it out to the festival this year. A couple friends of mine had films there. I try to make as many festivals as I can every year."

I started to get the funny feeling that Albert was a real person. I had expected him to be like Sammy Glick, but he seemed normal. Everybody at the party seemed normal. They were playing Yahtzee, fer the luvva Christ. They were laughing. What the hell kind of show-biz phonies were these?

"It was sort of an avant-garde film," I said. Then I said, "When I get back to Denver I could ask Toby to send you a tape of it."

"That would be great," Albert said. "I'd love to see it."

"Toby is a good filmmaker," Alicia said.

Albert grinned and reached around Alicia's shoulders and gave her a quick hug, then released her and looked at me. "Are you sure you can't stay a little longer? What time does your plane leave?"

"Oh, I don't know. I was going to try to catch an eight o'clock flight."

"Do you have a reservation?"

"No. I was just going out to LAX and hop the first plane home."

"Well listen," Albert said, "could you possibly take a flight tomorrow? We'd love to have you stick around for the party."

I looked at Albert, then I looked at Alicia, then I looked at myself. Of the three of us, I came off the worst. I didn't think I had ever met anyone quite as up-front as Albert. He was completely the opposite of what I had expected. I had seen too many movies. I reached into my back pocket and pulled out the VHS copy of *Summer Kicks.*

"I didn't come here to pitch a screenplay," I heard myself say.

Albert raised his eyebrows inquiringly.

"I came here to show this to Alicia and ask her to watch it," I said.

He looked down at the tape in my hand. "What is it?"

"It's a movie called *Summer Kicks*. It was produced twenty years ago."

Albert leaned toward the box. He squinted at the artwork. He was curious about the tape, I could see that. He was interested. For some reason I had gotten the idea that the only thing anybody in Hollywood was interested in was money. I was thrown off by the fact that Albert seemed interested in taxis and cranberries and Yahtzee and Toby. I was thrown off by the fact that Albert was real.

"Well hey, let's pop it on the machine and take a look at it," he said, pointing across the room. There was cassette player on top of the TV.

I took a deep breath and let out a sigh. "No. I don't think so."

"Why not?" Albert said.

"Because the star of this movie is Alicia's mother."

A small smile formed on Alicia's face. It was the kind of smile that people get when they think you're kidding but they're not quite sure, so they start to smile just in case. This always includes a slight frown, mostly involving the eyebrows. The frown/smile I guess you could call it. As good a name as any, and better than most.

"What do you mean?" Alicia said.

"When your mother was eighteen years old, she came out to Hollywood to become an actress," I said. "She got the lead role in *Summer Kicks*."

"She never told me that," Alicia said.

"I don't blame her," I said. "I watched this movie. It's terrible. Your mother didn't have any formal training as an actress. After the movie bombed, she went back to Denver and married your father."

Alicia stared at the thing in my hand. Albert didn't say anything. He kept looking from the cassette to Alicia's face and back to the cassette. Then he said, "Where did you get that tape?"

"From a video store in Venice called The Cult Hut."

"Oh yes," he said. "Everybody knows that place. They carry those hard-to-find videos."

I nodded and looked at Alice "This wasn't so hard to find, I guess. But I don't think I'm going to show it to you. It would just embarrass you in front of all these nice people, and I don't want to do that. You're old enough to make your own decisions, and it's clear to me that you're set on becoming an actress. I felt responsible for the fact that you ended up out here, and I've done my best to talk you out of making what I thought was a mistake. But that's all I have to offer. I'm leaving now. Good luck with your film career, Alicia. Thanks for the cranberry juice, Albert."

I slipped the tape into my back pocket. I turned and walked through the crowd of chatting, laughing people.

I stepped out to the patio and crossed to the wooden steps. I paused and took a look at the Pacific Ocean before I descended to the sand. The ocean looked just like the ocean in every beach party movie I had ever seen, including *Summer Kicks*. They say you can never step into the same river twice, but I had a feeling that didn't apply to oceans. Alicia was about to dive into her mother's ocean, and there was nothing I could do to stop her. If I ever saw Alicia Hightower in a movie, I figured my name belonged in the credits under casting. I took a vow right then and there that as long as I lived, I would never again get involved in the personal lives of my fares.

I drove to Santa Monica and returned the tape and player to The Cult Hut. After getting my three-hundred-dollar deposit canceled from my credit card, the entire cost of the bash came to twelve dollars. About the same as cab fare from Stapleton International Airport to the Brown Palace Hotel back in the days before DIA opened behind schedule and over budget.

CHAPTER 26

I slept that night at the Piedmont, then took a plane out the next morning. It was snowing when we landed at DIA. Three inches on the ground. Business was so good that taxis were doubling up on fares. There was a chance that even Big Al would be working the airport. I knew the odds were against it, but Big Al had a feel for long shots and I didn't want to face him, even if those odds were worse than my winning the lottery. It would be just my luck to hit the jackpot on this of all days. I stood inside the airport terminal looking through a window at the moving line of cabs until I figured I could hop a ride in something other than a Rocky.

When the long line of taxis pulling up at the door became an unbroken yellow, I carried my luggage outside and told the starter where I was going. He paired me with an old lady who was headed for a hotel downtown. I told the driver he could drop her off first, even though it would have been cheaper to let me out first. But that was okay with me. I wasn't that eager to get home. I wanted to sit in the back of a taxi for the rest of my life and let somebody else take charge of the world. I was no good at it.

The old lady introduced herself and told me she had come to Denver because her niece was going in for an operation. I wasn't driving this hack, so I simply nodded without interest. But the driver perked up and asked about the operation. I didn't blame him. A tip hung in the balance. For the next half-hour the driver and I got a detailed description of a spleen operation that the old lady had undergone when she was somebody's niece.

The driver dropped her off at the Hilton. After he got back in and pulled away from the front door, he glanced back at me and said, "Your name is Murph, isn't it?"

I nodded.

"You drive for Rocky, don't you?" I nodded.

When he didn't expand further upon this line of inquiry, I leaned toward the front seat and asked why he was asking.

"The Word is out on you," he said.

I froze.

"What Word?"

"The girl that everybody thought you murdered last week," he said, "she's still in Hollywood, isn't she?"

I sat back, closed my eyes, and bowed my head. Only now did I remember that I had forgotten to dwell upon my sins during the trip home. I had been too busy watching the in-flight movie, although I did manage to eat three sacks of peanuts.

"How did you know?" I said.

"The Word got around," he said. "The Word always gets around."

I knew this as well as he and every other cab driver on the planet.

Then he said, "Someone made book on it."

"On what?" I said.

"They bet that you'd fail to talk her into coming home." He glanced at me, then at the empty spot beside me, and grinned.

When the driver turned back to face the approaching panorama of Capitol Hill, I said, "Here's some inside info. As soon as you can get to a phone, bet every dime you've got against me. You'll make a fortune."

When we arrived at my apartment building, I pulled out my billfold, but he waved it off. "Keep your money," he said. He was still grinning.

I looked him in the eye. I read what was in those eyes. In my line of work, and in my rear-view mirror, you see a lot of eyes. I read greed, joy, and thanks, in alphabetical order.

I closed my billfold and got out. He hopped out and opened the trunk for me. I hauled out my suitcase, then looked him in the eye. "You got maybe an hour before every cabbie in Denver knows I'm back," I said. "You better get to a phone fast. There's a 7-11 right down on Colfax."

"I know it," he said.

He was already headed for the driver's seat. I watched as he pulled away. Our encounter made me feel sort of good inside. It made me feel like my life wasn't a total waste. I had just given the last best advice I would ever give, and someone was going to clean up betting against me. I felt redeemed.

I trudged up the back fire escape and entered my crow's nest. The telephone was ringing.

I let it ring. I intended never to answer my phone again as long as I lived.

After awhile it stopped ringing. Sooner or later phones always stop ringing. That's the only good thing I can say about telephones.

I checked my wristwatch against the digital numbers that appeared on my cable box, the clock by which I lived my life. It was a few minutes past noon. My wristwatch was still set on Hollywood time, so I set it back to Loser time.

I check the cable-TV clock every Sunday night to make sure my wall clock is in synch. Prior to the invention of cable I was not always in synch with the movement of the stars and planets, but now I am. That may sound like something bordering on neurosis, until you consider the fact that I have never miscued a VHS recording. When I die, I fully expect to die exactly on time. I imagine that prior to the invention of the electric clock, a lot of people died when they weren't supposed to.

I was in the middle of cooking a hamburger when the phone started ringing again. I gritted my teeth. I felt like I was back in grade school, getting called on by a relentless nun. But the beauty of this nun was that

I could ignore her. The problem was, I couldn't shut her up—just like a real nun.

I finally slammed the spatula down on the counter and went into the living room and picked up the receiver. "Hello!"

"Murph?"

"What!"

"This is Alicia Hightower."

"Oh." I had a good head of steam built up, but this drained my radiator. "Alicia," I said. "Is something wrong?"

"No," she said. "I'm glad I caught you at home. I've been trying to call you."

I was aghast. Turns out she was the one calling when I entered the apartment. Had I known that, I would have picked up the phone. There was no way I could win in this world. Every decision I had ever made was wrong.

"I just walked in," I lied. "What's up?"

"Murph, I just wanted to thank you for helping me," she said. This made me feel worse. She seemed to think I had done her a favor. Normally this was what I wanted people to think, especially if a large tip hung in the balance.

"You're welcome," I said, my voice withering. I meant it, but I felt like I was still in the process of lying.

"And I want to ask you a favor," she said.

"Name it."

"Could you come pick me up?"

"Where are you?"

"At DIA."

"DIA?" I said. "But … but … but … but."

I actually said that. I said "But … but … but … but." It was the only time in my life I had ever said that.

"I came back to Denver," Alicia said. "And I wonder if you would come out here and pick me up. There's something I want to tell you."

After I hung up the phone I went into the kitchen and turned off the flame beneath the frying pan, leaving my hamburger half-cooked. It gave me the willies.

Ten minutes later I was seated in my Chevy with the hood ornament aimed at Denver International Airport, more-or-less. I took Colfax to Colorado to I-70. Within twenty minutes I could see the tent-like roof of DIA through the falling snow. It made a pretty picture. Almost as pretty as Alicia Hightower standing at the curb on the pick-up level at DIA. The pick-up level is protected by a roof. There wasn't much traffic at the pick-up level. Most people were taking cabs home from the airport. Their friends were staying away due to the snow. You wouldn't think they lived in Colorado the way people stayed indoors during snowstorms. But then most people in Colorado aren't asphalt warriors. I think they're Californians.

After I put Alicia's suitcase in the trunk of my heap, I almost opened the right-rear door to let her sit in the backseat. Habit of course. I stopped myself and opened the shotgun door. Some habits are good, and some are bad. Most of mine are bad.

After I got seated behind the steering wheel, I looked at Alicia. Her face was flushed from standing out in the cold during the past five minutes. I had told her exactly how long it would take me to get to the airport, and I had gotten there exactly when I had said I would, but she told me she had come out five minutes early. I didn't mind so much. I don't believe half the things cab drivers tell me either.

"It's good to see you back," I said.

"It's good to be back," she said.

I had to take her word for it. We didn't talk during the few minutes it took to negotiate the toy highway from the DIA terminal and out to

Peña Boulevard, which would take us to I-70. The curving, sweeping road that leads from the terminal to the tollbooths has always reminded me of a Disneyland ride. Maybe it's the tent of the terminal itself that sparks my vivid imagination in the way my Maw always tells me that radio is supposed to do. The DIA roof sort of looks like the Matterhorn ride. I once rode the Matterhorn. I don't want to talk about it.

Habit kicked in again when I approached the tollbooths. I almost got into the taxi lane. Taxis bypass the civilian tollbooth at DIA. DIA gets our money when we pull away from the staging area. There's a separate tollgate just for us cabbies. It makes us feel "special." Don't get me started on feeling special. I could talk all day about how special the PUC regulations make me feel.

"You said on the phone there was something you wanted to tell me," I said, after I paid at the civilian tollbooth. Paying a toll just like everyone else made me feel unimportant.

Alicia twisted a bit to the left on her seat and sat with her back to the door. This allowed her to face me. I liked that.

"I want to tell you that I'm sorry I made you spend your money to come out to Los Angeles and try to talk me out of becoming an actress."

I opened my mouth to tell her that the trip didn't cost me a dime. Found money had paid my way to Hollywood. But I reminded myself that I was talking to an eighteen-year-old girl who seemed to have turned into an eighteen-year-old woman overnight. I didn't want to rain on her growth experience.

"Don't worry about the money," I said. "I had a good time in LA. It was like a vacation, and I never complain about vacations."

"I want to pay you back for the money you spent," she said. I liked that. But I didn't like it. Again, I decided to hold off. She seemed to want to apologize more than anybody I had met during the past … well … let's just leave it at "during the past." People tend not to apologize to me.

I glanced at her and gave a quick shrug with a slight sideways tilt of my head, indicating that she didn't really have to do that. I often mumble my body language.

"The reason I want to pay you back is because you were right," she said. "You left the party at Albert's house before I had a chance to tell you what he said."

"About what?"

"About my demo reel."

"What did he say?"

"He said the same thing you did. He said I had the looks to become an actress, and I had the potential, but I didn't yet have the talent. He told me that I would probably have to take a lot of acting classes before I could get any worthwhile roles."

"He said that?" I said.

"Yes."

"Albert said that?"

"Yes."

"Let me ask you something," I said. "Why did Albert agree to take a look at the demo reel in the first place?"

"When I first met him at the party, I told him that I had come to Los Angeles to be an actress, and that I had a demo reel. He told me that he would be glad to take a look at it."

"That's all?"

"Yes."

"He didn't make any promises?"

Alicia giggled. "You and Albert talk alike."

"What do you mean by that?" I said indignantly. Nobody had ever compared me to a gentleman before.

"At the party that night, Albert said he wasn't making me any promises. He just said he would be glad to look at my demo at his office if I brought it over. He has a screening room in his office in Century City. It's like a little movie theater. It's really cool."

Interesting statement. Most movie theaters today are like screening rooms. They're not at all cool. The day of the giant movie palace is dead and gone. Finito. Are. Eye. Pee. Adios, Babycakes.

"When did he break the news that you needed to polish your act?" I said.

"That same day. I guess I didn't take it very well. I sort of started crying."

"Sort of, or for reals?" I said.

"For reals. But he felt bad about it. He said he would introduce me around. A lot of the people at his Malibu house were just like me. You know … beginners? I guess that's one of the ways you make it in the movies, you meet people."

"That's one of the ways," I said. "They call it 'schmoozing.'"

Alicia gave up another giggle. "That's just what Albert said. Oh, that reminds me." She began digging through her purse. By now we had converged with Interstate 70 and were headed west. The snow had stopped falling. Most of the traffic on the road seemed to consist of taxis going to and fro. Who invented the word "fro"? Some LA phony who didn't have time to say "from"?

Alicia pulled a sheaf of papers from her purse and held it up for me to see. "Here's your screenplay. Albert asked me to give it back to you."

My eyes got as big as saucers, for lack of a better simile. But I didn't have time for similes. I was busy keeping my saucers on the road. I had forgotten about the screenplay.

"He said to thank you for letting him look at it."

"Did he like it?" I said.

Alicia crinkled her nose and made her mouth small like a chipmunk getting ready to bite an acorn—her upper incisors were showing. She tilted her head sidewise and shrugged her shoulders. I had no trouble reading her body language. But I will say this: it was the most talented rejection slip I ever got.

I started to tell her that I hadn't been serious about showing Albert the screenplay, and that it was only a ruse to crash the beach party. But I'll admit it. The moment I handed the screenplay to Albert, I experienced something akin to the electric thrill that Robert Preston once enjoyed when Gilmore, Pat Conway, The Great Creatore, WC Handy, and John Philip Sousa all came to town on the same historic day.

I took the screenplay from Alicia and set it on the seat between us. "Thanks," I said. "I'm fairly used to getting rejection slips," which was true—I was used to it in the way that World War I doughboys got used to living in muddy hell holes.

"I hope you weren't counting on it," she said.

This made me chuckle. Writers always count on, and never count on, their submissions. This is something that's difficult for non-writers and psychiatrists to understand.

"Nah," I said, tapping the screenplay. "There's plenty more where this came from," which was also true. Need I say more?

Yes. When we got to Colorado Boulevard, Alicia told me she wanted to go home. By "home" she meant her parents' home. I glanced at her inquiringly. I started to say something, but then remembered my vow to never again get involved in the personal lives of my fares. Even though I wasn't driving a taxi right then, I felt the vow still held. I'm not a lawyer so I don't use technicalities to weasel out of vows, unless I'm bored.

"I saw *Summer Kicks*," Alicia said.

I damn near lost control of my heap. "What do you mean?" I said. "When?"

"Last night. A little while after you left, Albert drove me to Venice and we rented the tape at The Cult Hut."

"Whose idea was that?" I said.

"Mine. Albert tried to talk me out of it. He told me that you said I would be embarrassed by it. He didn't want me to get my feelings hurt again. He let me watch the movie after the party ended and everyone else went home."

Whoa.

I suddenly felt myself getting suspicious.

"What do you mean ... everyone else went home?" I said. "When did the party end?"

"At sunset. Most of the people had to get up early to go to work, the ones with movie jobs anyway. We took the tape back to The Cult Hut when it was over, then Albert drove me back to Brenda's apartment."

I breathed a deep sigh of relief. I really do need an anger management course, or some kind of goddamn therapy.

"That's what I really wanted to thank you for, Murph. My mother was terrible in that movie. She looked just like me." Her voice faltered when she said this.

I glanced at Alicia. Her eyes were tearing up. I've always said that a taxicab is a terrible place to have an epiphany. Thank God we were in my Chevy.

"That's when I decided you were right." She took a deep breath and smiled at me. "That's when I decided to return to Denver. I'm going to go back to school, Murph. I'm going to college and become a theater major. I'm going to try to learn how to become a real actress. And I have you to thank for that."

I blinked a couple of times. My corneas seemed to be fogging up. I'll admit it. I'm a softie. But keep that under your hat. Someday I hope to have a reputation to protect.

Pretty soon we were cruising along east 8th Avenue where the "rich folks" reside, as I call 'em. As good a name as any, and better than most.

I dropped Alicia and her suitcase off at the front gate. I waited while she passed through the iron bars, went up the long sidewalk, and stepped through the doorway where her parents were waiting for her.

Okay. I'll admit it. I let Alicia give me a peck on the cheek before she climbed out of my heap. I normally don't allow taxi fares to kiss me at the end of a ride, but she was old enough to vote and I was off duty, all right? Give me a break.

CHAPTER 27

After I got back to my crow's nest I gave Toby a call. I told him that Alicia Hightower was back in town. I explained to him about the misunderstanding concerning the "stolen" demo reel. Then I described my visit to Hollywood, but I kept it brief. I gave it to him in what the professional screenwriters call a "treatment form," meaning I left out the embarrassing parts—such as my latest rejection slip.

As far as I was concerned, that was the last treatment form I was ever going to deal with. I was through with screenwriting. I was through with dreaming about Hollywood. I figured it was time to take some of the advice I had given Alicia and stop fooling myself. I was no screenwriter. I was going to stick with novel writing—at least until I deluded some young cab fare into going to New York City to try and break into the big time by hounding the editors on publisher's row and getting into a terrible fix, which would require me to fly to The Big Apple and bail him out and subsequently throw my Smith Corona into the trash. I gave it two months. Plenty of time to collect some good solid rejection slips with the words "Sorry, not for us" scribbled at the bottom by a twenty-one-year-old first reader.

I wanted things to get back to normal. There was still some money left in the demo reel fund, which I would have to return to Randolph Hightower. This, of course, ran counter to everything I had ever read about Hollywood accounting practices. But as I've said, I'm no lawyer. I wouldn't have the slightest idea how to hide a couple thousand bucks under a red line, short of stashing the dough in my copy of *Finnegans Wake* and waiting for the IRS to bust down my door.

I decided to hit the sack early that night. I was exhausted. I planned on driving 127 the next day. This was how I was going to get things back to normal—by working. I never thought I would use the words "working" and "normal" in the same sentence, but I'll try anything to avoid facing reality. I just wanted to forget the past couple of weeks. I finished cooking the hamburger that I had been manhandling when Alicia called. The willies returned briefly, but went away after the meat was browned through and through.

I ate the burger with a Coke while seated in front of my TV. I managed to catch the last ten minutes of *Gilligan's Island*. It was the episode where a rock group called the Mosquitoes came to the island. Their names were Bingo, Bango, Bongo, and Irving. Bango, Bongo, and Irving were really The Wellingtons, the band that had recorded the show's theme song, "The Ballad of Gilligan's Island." I'll admit it. I got choked up seeing them. It was like seeing a photograph of the real Elliot Ness.

Afterward I went into my bedroom, kicked off my Keds, and collapsed into bed. As I closed my eyes, I spoke aloud my vow to never again get involved in the personal lives of my fares. It felt funny to be talking out loud in the dark with my eyes closed, so after I finished the vow I started saying my name out loud. "Murph," I said. "Muuuurph." It was creepy. It made me feel like I was back in high school. Then I drifted into unconsciousness. That was like high school, too.

The next morning I drove my heap to Rocky Cab and parked in the lot. I grabbed my plastic briefcase and got out and entered the on-call room. The place was crowded with drivers getting ready to seize the asphalt, talking, joking, and lying about the great fares they had copped last week. But as I walked in, the place grew silent. Everybody glanced at me, then looked away. I liked that.

I walked up to the cage where Rollo was lethargically chewing on a donut. Due to the fact that it was his job to give me my key and tripsheet, he wasn't able to look away from me until we had transacted our business. I didn't understand what was going on, which suited me fine. I had found that the only thing worse than getting involved in the personal lives of my fares was talking to cab drivers.

I took my trip-sheet and key and walked back outside. Just before the door closed I heard someone grumble, "Do-gooder!" It made the hairs on the back of my neck prickle. But I ignored it. If I paid attention to every prickle I experienced on a weekly basis, I would be a bundle of nerves.

But then something else funny happened. I was parked at the gas pump at a 7-11 filling the tank when another Rocky driver pulled up. He was an old pro. I had known him for a long time, so I worked up the energy to give him a friendly wave. I never wave at the new drivers. It only encourages them. But the old pro took one look at me, put his cab into gear, and drove off. I felt slighted. But I ignored it. If I paid attention to every slight I experienced on a weekly basis, I might start thinking people were on to me at last.

After that I drove to the Brown Palace. There were three cabbies ahead of me in line. But after I got parked, all three of them started their engines and drove away. I assumed the drivers had jumped good bells and were off to grab some nearby fares, so I pulled up to the first space in line and settled in to wait for a customer to walk out of the hotel with luggage and hop into my cab for a trip to DIA. This is what cab drivers always think. Hope springs eternal when you're first in line at a cabstand.

Then Big Al pulled up behind me. I looked at him in my rear-view mirror, and my neck really started to prickle. He was smiling at me. I had never seen him look so grotesque. I started to get worried. I closed my paperback, shut off the AM radio, and got out. I walked back to his cab, wishing to God he would stop smiling. It was the kind of smile you see on the face of a gunslinger when a stranger rides into town.

He rolled down his window.

"You forgot to dwell on your sins, didn't you, Tenderfoot," he said. It wasn't a question, it was a blanket condemnation. I stood stock still and stared into his cab. It wasn't his smile that had my attention now. It was his open briefcase. It was filled to the brim with wrinkled dollar bills.

The kind of dollar bills taxi drivers keep stuffed in their shirt pockets. And suddenly I remembered.

"He's looking for me, isn't he?" I said.

Big Al nodded. He kept smiling.

"Where is he?" I said.

"Last I saw of him, he was cruising past the Hilton, eyeballing Rocky drivers."

I glanced up the street expecting a Yellow Cab to come barreling around the corner at any moment.

"Make my day," Big Al said. "Tell me you did that on purpose."

"You gotta be kidding," I said. "I never did anything on purpose in my life."

Just to be on the safe side, I climbed into the backseat of Big Al's cab and ducked my head down low.

"You're the guy who made book on me, aren't you?" I said.

"I gotta hand it to you, Tenderfoot," Big Al said. "I didn't doubt for a moment that you would bring that murdered girl back from Hollywood, but I never thought you would do it in style."

"That makes two of us."

"When the word got out that you were returning to Denver empty-handed, my telephone started jumping off the hook."

"What do you mean?" I said. "How did people know I was returning alone?"

"They got Yellow Cabs in Los Angeles, too," he said. "The drivers at LAX were watching your every move."

"Good Lord," I choked.

"And baby, you slipped one right past them."

"Y … y … yeah," I chortled nervously.

"Now all I have to do is keep you alive until the lynch mob disperses."

To make a long story short, Big Al had cleaned up. It seemed like every Yellow Cab driver in Denver had bet that I would return empty-handed, and apparently most of the Rocky drivers had taken a flyer on me, too. I don't know how many had bet their last dime, except the one Yellow driver to whom I had given my fabulous inside info. That was the worst piece of advice ever given out in the entire history of my mouth.

And then it happened. A Yellow Cab came racing around the corner and pulled up next to 127. The driver eyeballed my empty driver's seat, then jammed his cab into reverse and backed up. He pulled in behind Big Al's cab and honked his horn.

Big Al looked around at me. "Well, Tenderfoot," he said, "ask not for whom the bell tolls."

I took a deep breath and sighed.

"Want me to back you up?" he said with a note of disinterest in his voice.

"No," I said. I reached for the door handle.

"Murph," he said. He rarely calls me Murph.

"What?"

"Be a man."

"I'll try anything once."

The Yellow driver was hopping mad. He climbed out of his cab and came stomping right up to me. "You ... you ... you ..." he said. He really did.

"Lose something?" I said.

"You know damn well what I lost!"

"Your dignity?"

"You gave me a bum steer!"

"Welcome to Vegas."

"Why youu ...! I oughtaaa ...!"

"Did you ever see *The Sting*?"

"What!"

"*The Sting*. Robert Redford. Paul Newman. Robert Shaw. Won the Academy Award for Best Picture in seventy-three."

He was angry, but he was getting rattled. This often happens when people talk to me.

He nodded.

"You got stung," I said. "You got set up and knocked down. I took you to the cleaners. You were the easiest mark I ever pegged."

"You never did any such thing," he said, but there was a note of doubt in his voice.

"And when The Word gets out on the street that you were played for a sucker," I said, "you'll be the laughing stock of the Public Utilities Commission."

He started trembling. He reached into his shirt pocket and tweezered a cigarette out of his pack with two fingers, the way guys in the army used to do when they didn't want to share a pack. He opened a book of matches and tore off a paper match and tried to light it. The fool didn't even close cover before striking. But he couldn't get it lit. His hands were shaking too much. I reached into my shirt pocket and pulled out a Bic. Even though I don't smoke cigarettes, I always carry a lighter. You would be surprised at how many smokers don't carry lighters, unless you've been in the army. "Want me to smoke it for you?" we soldiers used to quip.

I held out my Bic and lit the cig for him.

"Personally, I think it would be calamitous for you if every driver in Denver ... and Los Angeles ... found out you were the victim of an elaborate, labyrinthian, and dare I say it, Byzantine sting. You might even end up ... branded."

He exhaled a lungful of smoke. I continued to deflate him. "My advice would be to pretend it never happened. And just to help you along, I'll pretend it never happened, too. That way nobody will ever know how you fell for my scam like a ton of bricks. You'll be able to hold your head up high when you drive, and with that handsome Yellow cap you wear, you deserve to hold your head up high."

His trembling ceased. He was just staring at me now.

"Here's another bit of inside info I would like to pass along to you," I said. "Never take advice from a cab driver."

He glared at me for a moment, then raised his cigarette and broke it in half. He dropped the ash part into the gutter, then put the other half back into the pack the way people do who are pretending to cut down on smoking. Without a word he turned away, got back into his cab, and drove off.

I watched him go. Then I walked up to Big Al's window.

"How did I do?" I said.

"Ton of bricks?" he said. "I thought English majors avoided clichés."

There was no pleasing Big Al.

"My back was to the wall," I said. "I didn't have time for creative writing."

"That might explain your rejection slips."

That was what he said, but I knew what he was really saying: "What did I tell you about getting involved in the personal lives of your fares?"

I nodded.

A man with a suitcase came out of the Brown Palace and headed for 127. I glanced at him, then looked down at Big Al. "See you on the asphalt."

I walked to my taxi, opened the trunk, put the man's luggage inside, and slammed the lid closed. Then I opened the rear door for my fare. After he climbed into the backseat I shut the door, opened the driver's door and got behind the wheel. "Where to?" I said.

"DIA," he replied.

Things were back to normal.

Oh yeah. I forgot to mention something. A couple days later I got a call from Randolph Hightower. Apparently he had been trying to get ahold of me during the previous two days, but I had either not been at home or was watching *Gilligan's Island,* and no telephone ever lived that got between me and Mary Ann. But for some reason I happened to pick up the phone that evening. I think I was drinking schnapps.

Alicia had told him everything about her Hollywood adventure. I had sort of been hoping she wouldn't mention the escapade to her parents. Hope springs eternal when it comes to guilt. I was prepared to hang up and move back to Wichita, but he told me that he and his wife were pleased at the way things had turned out. He said he had expected Alicia to do something like that sooner or later, and he was just glad I had taken it upon myself to go out there and set things right. That was his interpretation of reality. I kept my mouth shut. I ought to do that more often.

Then he told me that his wife and daughter had gone through some sort of reconciliation. Apparently the fact that Alicia had become aware of the existence of *Summer Kicks*, and had viewed it, resulted in what the psychologists call a "breakthrough," although I doubt the film critics would concur. Apparently the Hightowers themselves had gotten hold of a copy of the tape and watched it as a sort of family therapy, or else just for laughs, but the upshot of the deal was that Mrs. Hightower had joined an AA group and Alicia had put in an application to the drama department at the University of Denver. Apparently the two of them were facing up to their personal and professional shortcomings as some sort of mother/daughter team.

"I want to give you a gift of thanks, Murph," Randolph said.

"That's not necessary, sir."

"Never look a gift horse in the mouth, Murph," he said, but then he was a businessman and not an English major. "If you're going to be home during the next half-hour or so, I would like to send Jeffrey over with your gift."

Believe it or not, as much as I like to get free things, I hate getting gifts. I prefer to just sort of "find" things. Christmas drives me insane, but let's not get into that. I told Mr. Hightower that I would keep a lookout for Jeffrey.

Twenty minutes later the black high-bouncing four-wheeler pulled up to the curb outside my apartment building, and Jeffrey hopped out with a gift-wrapped package. He even saluted before he hopped back into his vehicle. That was one fellow who liked his job. I wondered if I would enjoy driving his vehicle. Probably not. I had sworn off wearing snappy uniforms the day I received my army discharge. Me and snappy have "issues."

To make a short story shorter, the gift turned out to be an answering machine with a cassette deck. I was flabbergasted. In my entire life I had never considered buying an answering machine. Why would I need a machine to do what I never do anyway?

After I got the gift rigged up to my phone though, I began to appreciate the beauty of the concept. I don't own too many gadgets. I'll be honest. If I wasn't born with it, you'll have to convince me.

Within an hour the phone rang. I listened with fascination as some stranger began talking. The recorder beeped and clicked and whirred just like Robbie the Robot. I felt like Morbius, the ruler of the planet Altara. Pretty soon the stranger hung up. One day later I had more than twenty recordings of strangers saying things to my machine. I can't believe so many people call me when I'm out driving 127. Who are these people? How did they get my number? And why would anybody want to talk to me anyway?

I never did erase any of the recordings. I have a box of tapes filled with voices. I sometimes put the tapes on my stereo and listen to them in between episodes of *Gilligan*. But it makes me wonder what people did in the olden days before the invention of the telephone. Did the telephone cause people to start talking more than usual? Did Alexander Graham Bell invent the telephone just so his wife would talk to someone else? Life is a mystery. It's been awhile since I got the answering machine, but I haven't called Mr. Hightower back yet to thank him for the gift. I'm still thinking it over.

THE END

THE HEART OF DARKNESS CLUB

BOOK 3 IN THE ASPHALT WARRIOR SERIES

COMING SOON

CHAPTER 1

I pulled into the cabstand at the Fairmont Hotel just as a call came over the radio. There were five cabs ahead of me at the stand so I figured I had better take the call. If there had been four cabs I would have settled in with my Coke and Twinkie and paperback book, but five cabs meant that the waiting time for a fare to come out of the hotel would have been too long in terms of the "Work/ Loaf Ratio" that I have spent fourteen years perfecting as a taxi driver on the mean streets of Denver. I won't bore you with a long-winded explanation of the "W/LR" save to say that it is an algebraic formula of such complex numeric subtlety that it can be understood only by mathematicians and hobos.

"One twenty-seven," I said into the microphone.

"Five sixteen Tremont," the dispatcher said. "Party named Trowbridge. He'll be waiting outside."

"Check."

I hung up the mike and pulled out of the cabstand and drove down the street. A couple of the taxis were Rocky Cab hacks. I knew what the drivers were thinking: Murph knows something. Whenever a cabbie jumps a bell from a cabstand, the other cabbies think he knows something. Vail trip, they think. A rich businessman going to Denver International Airport, they think. They think anybody fool enough to abandon the security of a cabstand must be hip to a jackpot. I like people to mistakenly assume good things about me. It enhances my rep.

It took one minute to get to the Tremont address. I saw the guy waiting outside the building, but he was no businessman. It's easy to recognize businessmen. They wear suits and vote Republican. It's true that this guy was wearing what could loosely be defined as a "suit," if you think of Bozo the Clown as wearing a suit. Unmatched sports jacket, baggy pants, and dusty shoes, plus unkempt hair. That's all you need to know. He was standing in the midst of what I took to be all of his worldly possessions. My heart sank.

Every so often I get one of those people. "Movers" as they are referred to by us cabbies, although they are not be confused with "movers-and-shakers." Movers are people who think a taxicab is Mayflower Van Lines. They are people forced by tragic circumstances to flee their current residence and find someplace else to live. Their modus operandi is always the same. They give a little wave signaling that they called the cab, then they begin loading your trunk with their stuff. They disappear into their apartment building and come out with more stuff. There's usually a shabby suitcase or two. My heart sinks when I realize I've got a mover on my hands because he or she usually has an apartment lined up not far away, so the fare comes to only three or four dollars. It's worse than a supermarket run, because shoppers rarely have as much stuff as movers.

But my heart goes out to these people even as it's sinking, which is scientifically feasible as I know from experience. Out-and-down, that's where my heart went when I pulled up to the curb. I couldn't tell if the guy was older than me. It's always a shock to find myself in the presence of desperate people my own age. When I was a kid I always assumed that bums, losers, and grandparents had to be at least fifty years old.

"I have a few more things inside," the guy said as he thrust his shabby suitcase into my trunk along with a cardboard box filled with the twisted remains of his life. I nodded. I knew the drill. There's nothing you can say. You know you're in for at least a half-hour of down-time, meaning you won't be jumping any good bells for the next thirty minutes. It's sort of like waiting for a bus to nowhere except you're the driver.

I watched the guy disappear into the building. It was an old nineteenth-century Denver building, a five-story, red brick joint that had an appointment with the wrecking ball. The upper stories were apartments, and the ground-floor space had been a lot of things in its time, including an X-rated magazine store. I knew this because when I was a student at nearby UCD, I sometimes walked past this building on the way to a bar after class, but I never had the guts to step inside. (The word around the English department hinted that the store traded in 1950s *Playboys*, but nobody knew for sure.)

When Trowbridge came back outside with his arms loaded down with more stuff I worked a pleasant smile onto my face, but he didn't look at me. He was embarrassed, I could tell—me and embarrassment are old pals. I didn't offer to help him carry any of his stuff. That's the unwritten code between cabbies and movers. It may sound cruel, but that's the way the game is played. The cabby pretends to be miffed, and the mover is required to feel embarrassed. It's his punishment for tricking the cab driver into playing Mayflower, because he knows he's not going to give you a tip, and so do you.

When I say the cabbie pretends to be miffed, the truth is that the cabbie really is miffed, but only at himself for getting roped into a lousy trip. Cabbies are like gamblers. They hate to lose, but you'll notice that they never walk away from the craps table. And do you know why? It's because they believe that after they drop off the short fare they will get a Vail trip to balance their bad luck. Does the phrase "God is on my side" ring a bell? The worst part of being a cabbie gambler is that, unlike a Vegas gambler or a dog-track gambler, cabbies always break even. By this I mean you can tear your hair out over a short fare or click your heels over a trip to Vail, but at the end of the fiscal year you still average seventy lousy bucks per day. Fifty, if you happen to be me. You can't win in this game, but you can't lose either. It's sort of like high school—you can loaf through four years or study your ass off, but in the end everybody is handed the same ol' sheepskin.

"Where to?" I said.

"Five-sixteen Curtis," he replied.

A two-buck trip tops—it was almost a record.

I once got a call at a motel on east Colfax where a woman was moving from her motel room to a room in a motel next door. It was my first experience with a mover and I was staggered. I was thirty-one years old. I was fairly new at cab driving. The woman was around the same age as me, I could tell. After I got over my shock and outrage, my heart went out to her. She really seemed embarrassed. I helped her carry some boxes. I didn't know the rules. The fare came to a dollar-sixty. After I dropped her off, I drove away wondering what she would be doing when she was forty-five. You already know what I'm doing.

I pulled up at the Curtis address. It was another old, red brick building. The meter came to two dollars and twenty cents. Trowbridge leaned over the back of my seat and held out a crisp new five-dollar bill. I took it and reached into my shirt pocket for change but he said, "Keep it," and waved a horizontal palm as if shooing away pigeons. This made me feel bad. The guy obviously had taken similar trips and knew how cranky some cabbies could get about short trips. Me, I keep my crankiness to myself. Short trips come with the territory— and there actually is something to the belief that the next trip might end up a Vail trip. By "Vail trip" I mean any long trip that will bring the average of this hour's take to fifteen bucks. Everything evens out in the world of cab driving, unfortunately.

I did hop out though and help remove some boxes from the trunk, just to acknowledge the 115 percent tip. But I only set them on the sidewalk. I knew this was what he would want without asking. I could sense that, in his own way, he was an old pro and did not need or want help carrying his stuff into his newest awful digs. He got right to work hauling the boxes into the foyer and setting them down and striding back out to retrieve the rest of his stuff. He knew his business.

"Need any help?" I said, just to bring closure to the tip.

"No thank you, I'm fine," he said. It had a practiced sound. I nodded and climbed back into 127 and drove away. As I pulled up at a red light, I took a deep breath and said with a sigh, "There but for the grace of God, etc." I sigh that quite frequently. I have no idea what my life would be like or what I would be doing for a living if it wasn't for cab driving, but I suspect it would involve manual labor. Who the hell invented cab driving anyway? A pharaoh?

As I wended my way back toward the Fairmont I began to wonder what age Trowbridge was. He could have been younger than me but not by much. Sitting in a cab all day doing nothing has helped me to age well, unlike, for instance, a farmer battling hail and cows. Trowbridge had looked old, but that was partly due to his clothes and wild hair and four o'clock shadow. I myself sport a ponytail. The chicks tell me it makes me look younger. My male friends say it makes me look like I'm not "with it," meaning ponytails are "out" and have been, I guess, since the Sixties. But after disco was invented, I pretty much lost interest in American cultural innovation. For some reason, I still feel the same age I was when I began driving a cab fourteen years ago. As I overtly implied, I'm forty-five years old. I'll never forget the day I turned thirty-seven. On that day I said to myself, "I'm the same age as James Bond." It was one of the biggest thrills of my life, so you can imagine how thrilling my life is.